Glory Be

AUGUSTA SCATTERGOOD

For Jane, my own sister and friend.

And for Ivy and Kate and Jay,
with appreciation.

Library of Congress Cataloging in Publication Data available

ISBN 978-0-545-33180-7
10 9 8 7 6 5 4 3 2 1   12 13 14 15 16
Printed in the United States of America 23
First edition, January 2012

The text is set in Adobe Caslon, and the display font is PastonchiMT.
Book design by Elizabeth B. Parisi

Contents

HANGING MOSS, MISSISSIPPI

JUNE 1964

Chapter One

COULDN'T HARDLY SPIT

What was taking Frankie so long?

We needed to hurry.

Franklin Cletus Smith has been my best friend since we hunted doodlebugs together in my backyard. Some people call him Frankfurter 'cause he's got hair the color of a hot dog. I call him Frankie. I squinted down the sidewalk, and finally here he came, dragging his towel with his bathing suit hiked way up.

"It's a million degrees out here. I've been waiting forever."

"Well, hey to you, too, Glory," he said.

I stood up and grabbed my swimming bag. "Where've you been?"

"I cut through Mrs. Simpson's backyard." He wiped

the sweat off his glasses with the bottom of his T-shirt. "Then I had to turn around and run down the alley when her mangy old hound dog took off after me."

"Don't worry about that dog," I told him. "He's half blind. Just barks at what he can't see."

"Some dogs run forty miles an hour." He announced that like it was the gospel truth. Frankie was always saying stuff that sounded like it came straight from his World Book Encyclopedia.

"Let's go," I said. "It's so hot I can't hardly spit. Jesslyn's already at the pool. She might up and decide she's bored, and leave before I put my big toe in the water."

I scratched at a mosquito bite and tugged at the bathing suit under my shorts. The backs of my legs were burning up from sitting on the concrete bench outside the library. I couldn't wait to feel the water's coolness, to dive in and flutter-kick all the way to the shallow end.

Frankie yanked at his towel. "I hope the pool's even open," he mumbled.

"Wait a minute," I said. "It'll be open. I'm going swimming. Why would they close the Community Pool now, when everybody needs a place to swim?"

"I heard something." He stared up at a noisy mockingbird perched in the shade tree in front of the library. Anybody watching Frankie would have sworn that mockingbird was the most interesting critter in the universe. "About cracks needing fixing."

"Nobody's closing our pool. Where'd you hear that?"

"My daddy. But it's a secret," Frankie answered, and headed off like he hadn't said a thing.

"Your daddy? What does he know?" I raced after him, all the time thinking why in tarnation would our pool be closing on the hottest day of the summer, just twelve days before the Fourth of July, my twelfth birthday? And what was the big secret anyhow?

Chapter Two

SPYING

HANGING MOSS
COMMUNITY POOL RULES
1. Open 9 AM–7 PM. Everyone welcome.
2. No one under the age of twelve allowed
in without supervision.
3. No horseplay.

"See there, Frankie. Your daddy doesn't know everything. Still open." I read the sign on the fence gate for the umpteenth time. "You suppose they'll ever change that rule that makes my bossy big sister in charge? Jesslyn can't swim half as good as me. Just because she's fourteen — and I'm only eleven — what difference does it make?"

"You know, Glory, nobody has to know how old you are. You can sneak in." Frankie looked around to see if anybody was watching us. "Like me."

"Not hardly. Since my daddy's been the preacher at First Fellowship United Church for my whole entire lifetime, half the people in this town know how old I am." I untangled a quarter from my bathing cap and dropped it on the sign-in table. "Let's go," I said, and followed Frankie to our special place near the back fence. We sat down on the grass.

I flipped my tennis shoes to the side of my towel and looked out at the pool. Eight ladies floated on their backs in a big circle, one foot in the air, then another, kicking away to some older-than-the-hills song blasting from the loudspeaker. "Look at that. The Esthers, hogging the pool again. Jesslyn says Mrs. Simpson named them after a movie star."

"My brother says Old Lady Simpson acts like she's the boss of the Community Pool." Frankie put his Archie funny book down and nodded toward the swimmers.

"All those ladies have green hair, you know."

Before he could quote from his fifth-grade science book about why chlorine turns hair green, I yelled, "Last one in's a monkey's uncle," and jumped up.

Frankie set his eyeglasses in his shoe for safekeeping. He took off the black-and-gold lanyard with a whistle hanging from it and laid it on top of his towel. Then Frankie fiddled with his swim goggles, and fastened on his pink plastic nose clip. Finally he slid into the pool, feet first.

I dived in the deep end, flutter-kicked over to Jesslyn, then climbed up the ladder. When I got out of the pool, I stood close enough to drip on her. "Hey, sis. I'm here."

Jesslyn turned from her pep squad friends. "I see you. Please move. You're blocking my sun." She slathered baby oil on her arm.

"Want a hot dog from the snack bar?" I asked. "I'll get you one. And french fries." Jesslyn looked at me like I'd offered her liver with onions.

Last summer, my sister taught me to hold my breath and swim the entire length of the pool underwater. Back then we sat on the same big towel while she painted my toenails pink. Not this summer. This summer Jesslyn is fed up with me.

I cannonballed back in, splashing Jesslyn and her snippy friends. When I got out, I headed for my towel. "Come on, Frankie," I told him. "We got us some spying to do."

Even underneath our favorite shade tree, it was so hot you couldn't hardly breathe. But when Jesslyn and her friends started whispering, and words like *cute boy* and *football player* and *two-piece bathing suit* drifted my way, I scooted my towel out from under that tree to get closer. They gossiped about her friend Mary Louise's party and talked about some new boy in town that Jesslyn seemed real interested in. The way those girls were studying their fancy-colored toenails, you would've thought they were paintings hanging in a museum.

When Frankie's brother, J.T. Smith, Mr. Football Hero, showed up, the toenail studying ended. Every single one of Jesslyn's pep squad friends started giggling and carrying on. Even with the sun beating down, J.T. had his varsity letter sweater slung over his shoulders. No swimming suit. I guess he was too good to go near the water. He had a toothpick hanging out of his mouth, a football under his arm, and the fiercest look on his face.

Frankie jumped up and ran over to where J.T. was. Maybe he thought his mean big brother was gonna make those boys playing Marco Polo, splashing left and right under the diving board, ask him to join in. Fat chance they'd let Frankfurter Smith play, even *if* his brother's the Hanging Moss Hornets' biggest star.

"You girls better enjoy this while you can." J.T. nodded toward the pool. He was grinning bigger than a cat trapping a mouse. "By next week, it'll be closed."

Jesslyn propped herself up on her elbows to look out at the turquoise water. "Closed? In the middle of the summer? You don't know what you're talking about, J.T."

"I know exactly what I'm talking about" was all he said.

When I heard that, I couldn't stop myself. I stormed over to Jesslyn. "Nobody will close our pool. It's almost July Fourth, the big parade and all." I started to say how it was my birthday and I'd had swimming parties here since I was little. But I didn't. I glared at Frankie's brother. "Why are you lying about our pool?"

J.T. spit out his toothpick and slicked back his black hair. "I ain't lying. You can blame it on them Freedom Workers. Those people from up North, in town to help the coloreds vote and swim in our pool. We don't need outside agitators down here making up new rules." J.T. started to move away from us. He was ending the conversation.

Jesslyn followed J.T. toward the gate, and I was right behind her. Her voice got so loud two lifeguards looked down. "Outside agitators? Do you even know what that means? You're just using big words. Before you start saying bad stuff about people, you should find out who these so-called outside agitators really are."

My stomach did a belly flop. Whatever an *outside agitator* was, it didn't sound good. I didn't understand what they were arguing about.

"Well, if you want to swim next to a colored person, go on ahead," J.T. hollered back at Jesslyn. "While you're at it, why don't you just hightail it across town to swim in their crummy pool?"

"Maybe I will," Jesslyn answered, quietly this time. But by now the entire pep squad was listening.

"What are you talking about, J.T.?" I looked up at him standing there, smiling to beat the band. "You don't know a thing."

"That's what you think," he answered. Then he strolled out of the pool gate like he owned the place.

For a minute everything got so still it felt like the entire Hanging Moss Community Pool was holding its breath, listening. After a while it was swimming pool noises again—mamas calling children, lifeguards' whistles, radios fighting with each other to see which one could make the most racket. Everything back to normal, seemed like.

I turned to Frankie. "Is something broken? Is that what you meant when you said the pool might be closing to fix stuff? Like a crack in the cement? Must be a teensy crack, right? Or that fence over by our mimosa tree? It's been broken ever since I can remember."

"Daddy told us it was closing," he answered. "My daddy's on the Town Council, you know."

"Yeah, well, as the preacher at First Fellowship my daddy knows as much as any old Town Council. He never said anything about this pool closing in the middle of the summer."

I kneeled down to peer into the pool water gurgling near the drains. Bobby pins, long hair, pink chewed-up bubble gum. No cracks.

I was trying not to care about swimming and splashing every single day for the rest of the summer in the cool water with Frankie, my one true friend. Or whether it mattered that Jesslyn just might be the laughingstock of the Hanging Moss Community Pool for hollering at Frankie's brother. Listening to J.T. talk just now, all the fun had drained right out of the Community Pool.

Chapter Three

LAURA LAMPERT COMES TO TOWN

*B*y the time I walked back to the shade tree, Jesslyn had packed up her towel and transistor radio. I slipped on my unlaced tennis shoes, grabbed my bag, and followed her out the gate. For the rest of the livelong day, Mary Louise, Mrs. Simpson, and the whole dang pool would be whispering about Jesslyn. But I was pretending like they had disappeared into the air like the sound of the lifeguards' whistles.

"Wait up," I said when I caught Jesslyn. "Wanna come to the library? We could read together."

She looked back at her friends. "I'm going home. The pool's not fun today," she said.

"You could help me plan my birthday party." I stopped to take a breath. So far, everybody was ignoring my birthday. Twelve days away and nobody cared a bit. "My party's before Mary Louise's. You think the pool will be open then?"

"I don't know, Glory. There's a lot going on around here that you're too young to understand. But I doubt the pool will close. And I don't have time to think about your party right now." Jesslyn turned and headed across the street toward home.

I didn't care if my sister ever helped me do a thing again. I'd figure this pool problem out. I walked straight to the library. Miss Bloom, the librarian, always knows everything. She'd know if the pool's got cracks in it.

I pushed open the door and caught my breath inside the big room. Old men sat at the long wooden tables, reading newspapers near the front windows. I looked for Miss Bloom. But what I saw, sitting in a cool, dark corner of the library with a book perched in her lap, was somebody I'd never laid eyes on, just about my age, who I swear didn't look like she belonged here in Hanging Moss. Instead of a ponytail like mine, one fat braid reached down to her waist. She wore heavy sandals, with socks. No kid in the entire state of Mississippi wore black socks in the summer. Shoot, if I wasn't standing smack-dab in the middle of the library, *I* wouldn't be wearing shoes.

I tucked my towel from the pool under me and scrunched down in a chair next to that girl's. I grabbed a book and turned the pages. Someone would have thought I was reading the most interesting thing in the whole wide library.

When I leaned over to see the cover of what the girl was reading, she jumped like I'd shot off a firecracker in the library. "That book good?"

Before the girl could answer, earrings came jangling and high heels clicking around the corner. Miss Bloom never was a librarian who went around shushing people.

"Gloriana, I see you've met Laura Lampert. She's visiting this summer. Just got to Hanging Moss yesterday." Miss Bloom smiled big as you please, then kept talking. "Her mother's starting a new clinic out from town; the Freedom Clinic we're calling it. For folks who don't have their own doctors or nurses. Laura's staying with me at the library while her mother works. Maybe you girls can come together tomorrow to help with story time." Miss Bloom took off her cat's-eye glasses to rub them clean with her fingers.

Laura smiled a little, then turned away quickly. I smiled back at her.

"What's that you're reading, honey?" Miss Bloom asked Laura.

"*The Secret in the Old Attic.* I love Nancy Drew books. I've read them all." When Laura Lampert said her *I*, it was in a Yankee voice like Walter Cronkite on the *Evening News*. And she ran her words together, real quick. Didn't talk a bit like I was used to.

But that didn't matter. "I've read every single Nancy Drew book in the entire world," I told her.

"Glory, why don't you show Laura around, outside where there's fresh air," Miss Bloom said. "Just don't be gone too long. Laura's mama will be back soon."

Fresh air, my foot. I was dripping sweat by the time we'd walked to the park behind the library.

"Are you staying all summer?" I asked her. "We could look for some story time books together in the picture book library tomorrow."

Laura spoke in such a quiet voice. "I'm not sure." I had to lean closer to hear her. "We drove from Ohio yesterday."

Ohio! Wait till I tell Frankie. I'd have to get him to look that up in one of his encyclopedias.

"I've never met a real Yankee before," I said.

Laura scrunched up her forehead, like she didn't know what I was talking about. "I live across the street," I said. "Maybe you could come to my house while you're here visiting from Ohio."

When we stopped in front of the swing set, I kicked off my shoes to feel the cool grass. There was sun shining on the slide. Its heat made that thing about to burn up. I moved under a shade tree near the little kids' pool. "See that?" I pointed toward the wading pool. "Don't ever swim there," I told Laura. "My friend Frankie and me have a pact to never even put a big toe in the Pee Pool." Kids splashed water and threw beach balls at each other. One of them was naked as a jaybird, standing by the side crying for his mama. No, sirree, you would not catch me in that baby pool full of pee. "Come on," I said. "I'll show you a statue. Supposed to be somebody famous."

Laura followed me across the street to the County Courthouse, still not saying much of anything. That didn't stop me from talking, though. I pointed up to the big statue of the soldier.

"Frankie claims he was killed in some battle while riding his horse. 'Course, I don't believe everything Frankie says anymore. He's been telling me a lie about our Community Pool closing. We swim there every single day." I wiped my sweaty forehead with the back of my hand and looked over at Laura in those black socks and sandals. Didn't look like she cared much for swimming pools. "You thirsty?" I asked. "Not much to drink around here but water unless the sno-cone truck comes by."

"Water's fine," Laura said. Boy was this girl quiet. She hardly talked.

I stepped up to the tall fountain next to the Courthouse, letting the water drip down my chin, dribbling it on my wrists to cool me off. I guess I must've taken too long because before I knew it, Laura was standing at the *other* fountain.

Oh, no! I had to do something quick.

"*Laura.*" I tugged at the back of her shirt. "That's the wrong fountain. Can't you read? See the sign?" I pointed to *Colored Only*, big as you please, written above the fountain where she'd just leaned her white face and took a long drink.

Laura stepped back and looked up at the signs above our two Courthouse fountains. She touched one fountain, then the other, turning the handles to make an arc of cold water.

"My mother told me about this," she said. "But they both work fine. It doesn't seem right."

Just then a little colored girl walked up and sat down on the hot sidewalk. When she splashed her white leather sandals in the puddle that had leaked from the fountain, all I could think was how mad her mama was gonna be when she saw the dirt she'd stirred up.

Out of the blue Laura asked that colored girl, "Would you like a drink? Do you need someone to lift you up to reach the water?" She held the girl up to the white people's fountain to take a sip! I stood there with my mouth hanging wide open.

As long as I'd been alive, there were two fountains side by side here across the street from Fireman's Park, where I played most every single day of the summer. One was for whites only, the other for coloreds. That's the way it always had been, and here this Yankee was helping a little colored girl drink out of the wrong fountain.

I looked across to the park. Had anybody caught us breaking the rules?

"Ruth Ann! Get on out of there." The boy hollering at the little girl must have been her big brother because he grabbed her hand and jerked her away from that whites-only fountain quicker than anything. He held that little colored girl's hand, tucked his chin, and took off. He turned around once, making sure we weren't chasing after them.

Laura looked from the fountain to me and back again as the colored boy and girl disappeared around the corner.

"What difference does it make which one we drink from?" Laura asked. "The water tastes the same." And she stepped up to the *wrong* fountain to get herself another long drink.

Oh, boy. I had a lot to teach this girl about Hanging Moss, Mississippi.

Chapter Four

ME AND EMMA AND NANCY DREW

*T*he next afternoon Jesslyn was upstairs with our bedroom door slammed shut, playing a sappy Elvis song on her record player. I plopped down in a kitchen chair to watch our cook, Emma, fixing supper, same as she'd done almost every single day since I was born.

She poured sweet tea into a tall jelly glass full of ice cubes. She sat next to me and stirred milk and two spoons of sugar into the coffee in her plain white cup. When she handed me my tea, I pressed our palms together. "Look here, Emma," I said. "My hand's the same as yours."

She shook her head and laughed. "Glory, sweetie, our hands aren't a thing alike. But they match up pretty good."

I looked hard at our hands together. Emma was right—they *were* different. Mine were getting nearly as big as Emma's, but her hands were the color of her coffee. Mine were white as Wonder bread. Still, Emma and me, we fit together like that Praying Hands statue over at Daddy's church.

When Emma pulled our hands apart, she slid a postcard across the kitchen table. "I saved you this, to mark the place we stopped reading our Nancy Drew book," she said. "Came from one of your daddy's church people. Says here on the back, they were visiting in Tennessee."

"'See Rock City,'" I read out loud. "Maybe someday I'll see Rock City," I told Emma. Right now, I could count on one hand the places Jesslyn and me had been. "This postcard's nice. I'm putting it in my Junk Poker box," I whispered, then I smiled at Emma. "To bet with."

"Don't let me hear you talking about betting, Glory. Your daddy, Brother Joe, will skin you alive if he catches you and your sister playing that Junk Poker card game. And betting! That goes against your daddy's church teaching." Emma stood up, opened the icebox, and put the fried chicken inside, for later.

Ever since our mama died, before I could hardly remember, Emma'd been worrying over Jesslyn and me.

Eat your green beans. Stay inside with the shades pulled down when it's hot. Watch crossing that street. Mostly, I paid attention and did what Emma said. But when it came to Junk Poker, that was different. I tucked the postcard into our Nancy Drew book to save for my next card game with Jesslyn.

To get Emma's attention onto something else, I said, "Guess what, Emma. I met a girl at the library. Her name's Laura and she's from up north. She drank out of the wrong water fountain over at the Courthouse. I told her not to but she wouldn't listen."

Emma didn't answer. She was listening, though.

"Reckon she'll be my friend? She doesn't talk much, and when she does, she talks funny 'cause she's a Yankee. Miss Bloom says her mama's here being a nurse. You heard of a place out on the highway, called some Freedom Clinic thing?"

Emma shook her head. She still wasn't talking, so I started on something new. At least her mind was off my Junk Poker postcard.

"Frankie says the pool's gonna close," I told Emma. "He says it's a secret. Claims there's cracks needing fixing or a broken fence. You think there's cracks in our swimming pool?"

I could see Emma's jaw twitching. She was trying hard not to say something. She stood at the sink washing her coffee cup over and over like the Queen of Sheba might be coming to our house for a tea party.

When Emma finally turned around, I stood up and crossed my arms across my chest. "What?" I stuck my chin out. "Are you mad at me?" I asked her.

Emma reached out and put her arm around my shoulders. "I know about that clinic." Her voice was soft and low. "And I doubt your swimming pool has half the cracks as some pools I know about. But you stay clear of all that. Don't be worrying about what you can't fix, Glory honey," she said.

I grabbed our Nancy Drew book and stormed off.

Chapter Five

JESSLYN PITCHES A FIT

*T*hat night after supper, our daddy, Brother Joe Hemphill, head preacher of the First Fellowship United Church, took his second dish of cherry cobbler to the front porch to practice his sermons for preaching on Wednesday night and next Sunday morning. Emma was nowhere to be seen. And it looked to me like Jesslyn was up to no good.

"Why'd you do those dishes all by yourself?" I couldn't hardly believe my eyes. She hadn't even asked me to help with drying. "Where's Emma?"

"Emma went home early." Jesslyn wiped her hands on the dish towel, slipped the pearl ring that used to be our mama's back on her finger, then turned around and gave me one of her looks.

"What for?" I asked. "Emma never goes home early."

"Something about company at her house." Jesslyn smiled at me like the world was one big happy family. "I wanted to help out."

If Emma had been standing in our kitchen right then, she would have been telling me, "Gloriana June Hemphill, you are too nosy for your own good." Even though Emma might call it snooping, I didn't believe Jesslyn would be washing and drying those dishes for the pure D. niceness of it. I had to be nosy.

Jesslyn pranced upstairs to our room. I followed her. While she primped in front of the mirror, I reached under my bed for my secret shoe box of treasures. Shells from the times we visited our grandma in Florida, two Jesus bookmarks I'd won at Vacation Bible School, my Cracker Jack whistle, a bag of collected bottle caps, ten copper pennies, wax lips. My new Rock City postcard. I'd saved it all to bet with.

"Wanna play Junk Poker?" I asked.

With the way Jesslyn glared, I might have well asked her to play Patty-Cake. "I've got better things to do," she said. "Besides, I dumped my shoe box out."

"What'd you do that for? You made up Junk Poker

when we were little, before I could hardly count to twenty-one and beat you. Now that I'm getting good and winning all your junk away from you, you don't want to play with me?"

Jesslyn smiled into her mirror, dug through the mess of lipsticks and bobby pins on her dresser, and pretended I wasn't in the room.

"Why're you getting so dressed up?"

"Mind your own business, Glory." She flipped up the curl of her hair and painted on Persian Melon lipstick. I untied the purple bow on my Buster Brown shoe box and lined up my Junk Poker treasures on the bumpy chenille bedspread.

Jesslyn smeared Vaseline on her eyebrows, a trick she learned from her stuck-up pep squad friends. Says when they march up and down the football field, shiny eyebrows give them "a movie star look."

I blew on my Cracker Jack whistle. "Where're you going?" I asked her.

"If you must know," she said, dabbing Evening in Paris perfume behind her ears, "to the library with Mary Louise. To plan her birthday party."

"Sure are getting fixed up for the library." I held a

shell up to my ear, pretending to listen to the ocean, biting my lip thinking about how Jesslyn didn't care one bit about *my* birthday.

Our daddy knocked real quiet on our bedroom door. I stuffed my treasures in my shoe box quick. "Everything okay, girls?" he asked. He never was one for much talk unless he was in front of pews full of people waiting for the Good Word.

"Daddy, now that I'm going to high school, I'm too old to be sharing a room with Glory." Jesslyn gave him her *I could never do a thing wrong* look. "She's bothersome. And messy. I want Mama's old sewing room."

Last summer when the ceiling fan stirred up the heat, Jesslyn and me had pushed our beds close together. During the night we kicked off our sheets and flipped our pillows to the cool side. Finally we gave up on sleep, pulled out our secret shoe boxes, and played cards. Now here she was tossing out all her junk for our game and wanting to move to the sewing room!

"I'm *not* messy." I straightened the perfect spines of my Nancy Drew books standing like soldiers on my shelf. "Look at Jesslyn's stuff." Mascara wands and hairbrushes, perfume bottles and powder boxes were piled on a stack of dog-eared movie magazines.

Jesslyn gave me the eye—again. "I have private things." The way she said *private* made me want to yank open her dresser drawer and steal her diary.

"Besides, Emma uses the sewing machine in there," I said. "There's just that little bed. With my quilt on it. You can't have my quilt."

"Now, girls, don't start fussing." Daddy raised a hand to hush us. "Let me think on this," he said, heading back to his sermon.

"I'm fixing to walk over to the library," Jesslyn told him, smiling. But our daddy was halfway down the steps already.

"I'm going with you." I pushed my Junk Poker box under the bed.

"You are not. Stop sticking your nosy self into my business." Jesslyn smoothed the wrinkles out of her skirt for the third time.

"How come we never do stuff together anymore? Last summer you bought me a diary for my birthday present and taught me how to jump double Dutch. Now you pitch a fit if I walk to the library with you."

"Mary Louise and I don't need you hanging around while we're planning her party." Jesslyn smiled in the mirror one last time and did a little dance down the stairs.

Mary Louise, my fanny. I peered in that mirror at my dishwater blond ponytail and tried to imagine myself in Persian Melon lipstick. Or my hair done up in Jesslyn's big brush rollers. Jesslyn's hair flipped up at the ends. Mine looked like it hadn't seen the right side of a brush all day.

I followed Jesslyn down the stairs, but the back door banged shut in my face before I could ask her any more questions.

I grabbed a Dreamsicle from the kitchen freezer and headed for the porch.

"Daddy, I'm going over to the library," I called.

He looked up from his Bible. "Be careful. It's getting dark out," he said. "And maybe you can walk home with your sister?" Then he picked up his pen and started writing on his sermon again.

"Yes, sir," I answered, wondering whether Jesslyn was even *at* the library.

I skipped down the front steps and headed off to find my sister.

Chapter Six

TWIRLING FIRE

I hid behind a giant oak tree and looked into the library window, then over toward Fireman's Park. Jesslyn was nowhere to be seen. I licked ice cream from my Dreamsicle off my fingers, wiped them clean on my shorts, and pushed open the heavy door into the library.

Still no Jesslyn.

I'd been helping Miss Bloom all summer so I knew my way around the library. I sneaked downstairs past the storerooms. I turned the corner near a box of old newspapers that stunk worse than dead catfish. Just as I was about to give up ever finding my sister, I caught a whiff of Evening in Paris. A rumbling floor fan made it hard for me to hear, but that was definitely Jesslyn's voice coming from inside a room down the hall. That was Jesslyn's perfume, too. Another voice chimed in that didn't sound one bit like Mary Louise Williams planning a birthday party. I pressed up against the wall, holding my breath.

"I love Elvis Presley. I have every one of his records," Jesslyn was saying.

"Me, too. But I had to leave them back in North Carolina when I left so fast," I heard a voice say. "Elvis and me—we even have the same middle name. Aaron. Did you know Aaron is Elvis's middle name?"

As if Jesslyn didn't own a scrapbook full of Elvis stuff and even a plaster of paris Elvis statue. She was liable to stand up and start singing "Love Me Tender" right then.

I held my breath and leaned around the door for a look. There was a boy with long sideburns! Sitting real close and talking to Jesslyn! I ducked back before they caught me.

"You look a little bit like Elvis," Jesslyn was saying. I almost gagged.

"Maybe we can drive up to Memphis to see Elvis's fancy house," the voice with the sideburns said. "Or maybe Tupelo, where Elvis was born. You reckon your daddy'd mind?"

Now as sure as I knew *my own* middle name, our daddy, Brother Joe Hemphill, would no sooner let his daughter drive out of town with a strange boy with the same middle name as Elvis than he'd let her fly to the moon.

"My daddy won't mind a bit," my sister said.

Lordy, Jesslyn was in trouble for sure.

I hurried out of the library, back across the street, and sat down at the kitchen table to drink a glass of cold milk. Daddy sat next to me, working on his crossword puzzle when Jesslyn waltzed in breathless like she'd seen the real Elvis.

"Hey, honey," Daddy said. "You get what you needed at the library?" He went back to his puzzle.

"Yessir, Daddy." She didn't even look at me. "And Mary Louise and I were talking just now. We need to go to Memphis to buy stuff for her birthday. And our batons for pep squad."

"Batons? Don't you already have a baton?" Our daddy glanced up but he kept his #2 pencil perched right on the paper so he wouldn't lose his place. "Do you know a six-letter word for a mythical creature?"

Jesslyn stood with her hand on her hip. She did that a lot lately. She didn't answer Daddy's crossword question. "The one I need is a fire baton. I'm learning how to twirl fire." She dragged *fire* out like she was about to star in Mr. Ringling's big-top circus.

Now, you'd think Daddy would have at least put his pencil down and thought a little bit about his oldest daughter traveling to Memphis to buy a fire baton, but no, he kept on worrying over that six-letter word for a mythical creature.

"I'll think on it," Daddy finally said.

"Mary Louise's cousin is driving. She's had her license for a long time," Jesslyn said.

"That her aunt Betty's girl?" Daddy knew most everybody in Hanging Moss.

My sister paused for one quick second before answering. "No, sir," she said. "It's somebody you've never met."

Chapter Seven

HERE'S WHAT'S BROKEN

*T*he next morning before anybody woke up, I pulled on my blue shorts and T-shirt from yesterday and tip-toed downstairs to talk to Emma. She was already singing and humming to herself, what sounded like a churchy song. Emma might have been old enough to be my mama, but she wasn't much taller than me, and her singing voice was high and tinkly. I stopped for a minute outside the kitchen door to listen. I dearly loved hearing Emma sing.

"What're you doing?" I asked.

Emma smiled. "Cooking biscuits. With bacon, like always." She took the bacon out of the icebox. "Where are you off to today, honey?" she asked.

I chewed on a hangnail I'd been working on all

week. "I wanted to go swimming, but Jesslyn's acting ugly, so maybe she won't let me come with her. Besides, what if the pool's already closed?"

Emma didn't answer. Just went back to turning the bacon in her black skillet. I twirled my ponytail and stared at a speck of dust on our red tabletop. My Nancy Drew book sat open to the chapter we'd been reading yesterday. I opened and shut it to the rhythm of Emma's quiet humming.

"Emma, you think something's really broken at the pool?" I flipped the book cover back and forth.

She got quiet before she answered. "What's broken is that some folks don't seem to like anything changing. Everything's got to stay the same in this part of town," she said. "I bet nobody ever thought how it's just as hot over where I live as it is where you live. Somebody ought to be fixin' that broken-down slab of concrete they call a swimming pool near me."

I shut my book. Emma didn't usually say stuff about her side of town and my side of town. I never even considered how she might not have a nice place to cool off. I *loved* our community pool—*my* pool, I liked to call it!

My pool had a snack bar, lounge chairs, swimming

lessons, and lifeguards. And I'd had my July Fourth birthday party at *my* pool most every year since I could swim. If I could remember back far enough, I even pictured my mama holding me while I put my face in the water for the very first time.

I started to ask more about Emma's pool, but when she poked a long fork into the bacon like she was spearing something hateful, I swallowed my questions.

Frankie showed up just when the bacon was cooling on the kitchen table. He'd come right through the back door and made himself at home.

"Frankie, do you hear bacon sizzling all the way down Church Street?" I asked him.

"Can just about smell it," he answered. He pushed his red hair off his forehead and straightened his glasses. "Smells good."

"Here. Have yourself one." Emma handed us toasted biscuits with bacon inside. Frankie and me sat on the back steps eating biscuits and licking butter off our fingers, being quiet together like we do sometimes. Then I got an idea.

"Hey, Emma. Can the girl I met at the library come to supper one night?" I called out. Emma could hear me through the screen door.

"Who'd you meet?" Frankie asked, stuffing the last bite in his mouth.

"A girl visiting from Ohio," I said. "Name's Laura. She likes Nancy Drew books, like me and Emma. Miss Bloom asked Laura and me to do story times together at the library. She says she doesn't have one single friend here. 'Cept me now."

Frankie leaned in, talked quiet so I could barely hear him. "Wonder if she's one of those troublemakers in town from up North," he said. "Here living with the coloreds. Trying to make them vote. Daddy says those long-haired hippies should stay where they belong. Plenty of people up North need help."

Frankie's daddy is the *James* in Bill and James' Wild West Wear and Clothing Emporium downtown. Besides selling cowboy hats and fancy boots, and telling Frankie what to think, Mr. Smith was once upon a time a big football hero. He still has old pictures and even his jerseys from a zillion years ago hanging all over his store.

"For your information, Frankie"—I stood up and looked right at him—"my new friend's not a trouble-maker and she's not living with any colored people. She's here with her mama. Laura Lampert, that's her name. Laura and me went for a walk. I showed her the Pee Pool and the playground and all. We might make us a lanyard or a friendship bracelet at the park tomorrow."

No use telling Frankie about the drinking fountains. I didn't want to give him another reason not to like Laura.

Frankie scrunched up his face, looked hard at a pile of red ants next to the steps. What he said next made my stomach knot up.

"I hate Yankees. You better be careful, Glory. My daddy says they're trouble."

Between his daddy and his mean big brother, J.T., somebody's always trying to tell Frankie what to think. Half the time I wonder if Frankie's scared to death of J.T. and of his own daddy.

"Does your daddy even know this girl from Ohio?" I asked.

Frankie didn't answer my question. I sat down again and glared, daring him to say one more thing about Laura.

"All those outsiders here in town might try to make us swim with colored children. And go to school with them. Daddy swears he'll yank me and J.T. out of school if a colored person's in my class."

About that time Jesslyn appeared at the back door. And even as quiet as Frankie talked, she'd heard him. She marched herself around in front of us on the steps.

"Just because somebody talks a little different doesn't mean you can't be nice to them." Jesslyn pointed her pink-painted fingernail at Frankie, then at me. "You think the world would come to an end if you had somebody not exactly like you sitting beside you in school next year?"

"We know plenty of different people. We don't mind sitting next to them." I didn't like Jesslyn thinking Frankie was hateful or stupid, but he was sure acting that way.

Jesslyn looked hard at him. "Some people in this town—your brother included—need to learn a thing or two about getting along with people." She stormed inside.

"Frankie, what you said, that was about the dumbest thing I ever heard of. Not going to school just because of who's sitting next to you? What about mean Donnie Drake who steals your homework? Or Kenny. He's been in our class since kindergarten. He smells like a billy goat and picks his nose. But you sit next to *him*."

Frankie wiped butter off his fingers onto his T-shirt

and shrugged his shoulders at me. "That's not the same."

"'Cause they're white? That's what your daddy thinks."

Frankie ignored that. "What's that girl doing at the town library anyhow? Daddy says pretty soon they'll be letting just anybody come in there." Frankie stood up and brushed the crumbs off his T-shirt. "Why do you like that Yankee?" he asked.

"I told you, her name's Laura," I said. "Call her by her name. She's nice, and we both love Nancy Drew books, and she needs a friend. She stays at the library while her mother's a nurse working somewhere out on the highway. Least that's what Miss Bloom told me."

What I didn't tell was about Laura's mother running that clinic, helping poor people who don't have any such thing as a doctor or a nurse. And if Miss Bloom says there are people who need this Freedom Clinic thing, whatever it is, then it's true.

"I like knowing somebody from Ohio," I said.

"My brother claims they talk and dress funny. And those freedom people try to make people do stuff they shouldn't."

Freedom people? Wasn't freedom something good? What was Frankie talking about?

But before he could tell me another lie that his brother or his daddy swore was the gospel truth, my daddy pushed open the back screen door.

"I'm going over to the church," he announced. "See you in a while, Glory."

"Thank you for having me to breakfast, Brother Joe. I sure do love Miss Emma's biscuits." Even when he wasn't exactly invited, Frankie remembered his manners.

"You're welcome anytime. Oh, and Glory, did I over-hear you talking about a visitor girl you met at the library just now? Invite her to supper, why don't you. You and Jesslyn can get to know people from other places." Then Daddy headed across to the church.

"I'll invite Laura Lampert to supper." I smiled real nice at Frankie. "My sister and I will know somebody from far off."

That is if Jesslyn would pull herself away from her new boyfriend long enough to pay me any nevermind. Or stop believing that trying out lipsticks with Mary Louise is more fun than playing Junk Poker with me. Then maybe Jesslyn would think having my new friend from Ohio over here to supper was fun.

Frankie let out a big sigh. "My daddy's gonna be mad," he said, and scooted home, kicking a rock halfway down the block. "My brother's gonna beat me up for playing with somebody who likes Yankees," he yelled back to me.

J.T. was scary all right, and I hoped he wouldn't beat Frankie up, I truly did. But right now I needed Frankie about as much as I needed Jesslyn's fancy orange lipstick.

"Emma, I'll be back real soon," I hollered over my shoulder. "I'm going to the library to invite Laura Lampert to supper."

From inside the kitchen, Emma shut the icebox door so hard, the milk bottles rattled.

Chapter Eight

LETTERS TO THE *TRIBUNE*

The next night before suppertime, Emma wiped her hands on her apron and stood back to admire her creation. "I hope your new friend likes this chicken spaghetti casserole."

"All Yankees like spaghetti," I said. Of course, I didn't know one single Yankee except Laura. I thought for a minute. "I hope Jesslyn won't act snotty to us because we're only eleven," I said.

"I'll make sure Jesslyn behaves." Emma picked up the big silver knife to swirl the last bit of icing onto a sweet-smelling cake.

"She's not always nice to me these days," I said. "And she argues with Daddy."

Emma pointed her knife to the ceiling, as if Jesslyn

could hear. "That girl would argue with a signpost. But your sister's just growing up. She'll be back to playing with you in a while, Glory."

"She wants to move into Mama's old sewing room. And you heard her fussing at me and Frankie, about his daddy and all," I said. "Jesslyn claims I don't know a thing about what's going on around here this summer."

Emma raised one eyebrow and shook her head. She reached into the cupboard for the dishes with little blue birds on them. "Extra folks coming and going don't make this kitchen any cooler. Get on out there and set the table, but be careful with these." She set the plates down gently. "Your mama's best china, special for tonight." Then she opened the refrigerator door and stood there fanning her face with her apron.

I wanted to edge in right next to her to cool off, but I could take a hint. I moved to the dining room just as Jesslyn tromped downstairs with big rollers in her hair. "Are you wearing those to the dinner table?" I tried to ask Jesslyn nicely.

"I'm going to the library after supper. To get a book," she answered like it was the stupidest question in the entire universe.

To see that boy again, I thought, when Jesslyn headed

back upstairs to her floor-length mirror. I didn't say a word, though. I liked knowing secrets, and for now I was working hard at keeping this one.

By the time my sister prissed back downstairs with her hair looking like she'd stepped out of the beauty parlor, Daddy and I were on the front porch swing. When a car stopped at the curb, he put down his newspaper. I waved to Laura, who was taking baby steps over the cracks in the sidewalk. A lady who must be her mama stepped out of the car.

"Hey, y'all. Come meet my daddy, Brother Joe Hemphill. He's the preacher over at First Fellowship United Church."

Daddy put out his hand to welcome her. "Laura, pleased to meet you. Is this your mother?"

"I'm happy to meet you, Reverend Hemphill. Miss Bloom has spoken highly of your family." Laura's mama talked funny like Laura, but the smile creeping across her face made me think I wouldn't even mind being sick if she could be my nurse.

"Can you stay for supper?" Daddy asked her.

"I'm late for my meeting," Mrs. Lampert said. "Thank you. Some other time?" She turned to give Laura a hug before she walked down the sidewalk and opened her car door. "I'll pick you up after dinner," she called back.

"At nine thirty sharp." Laura glanced down the street one more time, then followed me inside.

"This is my sister, Jesslyn," I introduced. "And Emma." Emma nodded Laura's way.

Jesslyn looked Laura up and down, from her long braid to her heavy brown sandals with black socks. But she didn't say anything bad. Once in a blue moon, Jesslyn could be nice if she tried.

The way Laura stood off to herself, with her hands folded tight in front of her and her lips pressed close together, it seemed like maybe she wasn't used to meeting new people. Especially the family of somebody she'd first laid eyes on in the library two days ago. Maybe she just didn't like Hanging Moss yet.

I aimed to change that.

"Supper'll be ready soon," I told Laura. "Wanna see my room?" She nodded and followed me upstairs. I did all the talking. "That's my mama's old sewing machine." I looked inside the room where now it was Emma who made our Halloween costumes and our curtains. "I don't hardly remember my mama, but Emma made me that quilt in there with reminders of when I was a little girl."

I kept on walking and talking, hoping Laura would say something pretty soon.

"This is my room, and Jesslyn's. All that messy stuff's hers." I pointed at the jumble of lipsticks and mascara falling off Jesslyn's dresser. "Don't know why she minds sharing a room with me, but she does. She claims she's moving to the sewing room." I picked up a white boot with a tassel on it and held it up. "Pep squad. She and her friends march around the football field wearing these and twirling batons. Do you have a sister?" I asked.

Laura shook her head. "I don't have brothers or sisters," she said. "A big sister would sure be fun."

"It *used* to be fun," I said.

When Laura picked up *The Secret of the Old Clock* from my row of books, she turned the pages so carefully I couldn't help but wonder if she planned to hide in my room reading all night. I needed to quick-like make her glad to be here. I took the Buster Brown shoe box from under my bed and slowly untied the purple ribbon. "Wanna see my Junk Poker box?"

"What's Junk Poker?"

"A card game. Jesslyn and I made it up when we were little. We bet against each other with the stuff in our boxes." I spread my treasures on the bedspread. I tossed a jacks ball up and down, waiting for Laura to say something. But she'd barely glanced up from *The Secret of the Old Clock.*

"Folks over at the church, they don't exactly approve of cards. So Jesslyn and me, we've kept Junk Poker a secret from our daddy."

"My grandpa plays cards," she said. "He taught me games." When Laura finally put down the book, she moved next to me and picked up one of the conch shells. That got her talking.

"They say you can hear the waves crashing in there."

"You're holding my favorite," I told her. "I'm never betting that shell."

"My mother promised we'd be going to the beach this summer, but we ended up coming here to Hanging Moss instead." Laura held my shell up to her ear. "Some days, wouldn't you like to disappear into the ocean inside?"

"The beach would've been more fun than this hot place. No water near here except the Pee Pool and the Community Pool. My friend Frankie swears that's about to close down." I sighed.

After a minute, Laura leaned back on the big pillows

lined up on my bed. "My mother keeps reminding me we're here to help," she said. "But staying the summer in a place where you don't know anyone and there's really nothing to do?" Laura's voice trailed off and she hugged the shell closer to her.

"You know *me* now," I said. Then I spied my record box filled with my new 45s, and I grabbed it off the shelf. "Hey, Laura. Ever heard of the Beatles?"

She put down the shell and scooted to the edge of my bed. "I love the Beatles! Did you see them on TV? Which one's your favorite?"

And after that, until Emma called us down to supper, all we did was sing along with my records, pretending we were John and Paul. All we talked about was how much better the Beatles sang than Elvis.

When Laura handed my shell back, I packed my treasures in the Buster Brown shoe box and hid it under my bed. I cut off the record player and put away my Beatles records.

Downstairs, Laura sat next to me at the dining room table, across from Jesslyn. Daddy took his chair last and bowed his head. "Bless this food, Lord, and those who have prepared it for us today," he prayed. "Watch over Laura and her mama and all the visitors here in Hanging

Moss. Thank you for your bountiful goodness. Amen."

It was finally time to eat.

From where I sat, I had a clear view of Emma in the kitchen. Pretty soon, she untied her apron and smoothed out her white uniform. When she brought the blue china casserole dish into the dining room and offered it to Laura, then to me, she looked like the ladies in the school cafeteria who watched every bite we took. Emma finished serving the spaghetti, then moved into the kitchen, but she was hovering, listening, right inside the door.

Daddy beamed around the table, tucked his big white napkin under his chin. Right off, he said, "I hope you like it here, Laura. If you haven't had a chance to go to the pool, or over to Fireman's Park, maybe you'd like to go with Glory one day."

Laura picked up her napkin and spread it in her lap over her skirt. She took one little bite at a time, chewed with her mouth closed.

Jesslyn broke her piece of hot bread in two. "Glory says your mother's a nurse."

"My mother works at the Freedom Clinic." Laura sat up straight. "It's for Negro people who don't have doctors." She scooted mushrooms from the spaghetti sauce off to one side of her plate, twirled a noodle, picked at a bite of chicken.

Any minute now, I expected Emma to call out, "Laura Lampert, stop playing with your food!" like she'd do if that was me twirling and scooting. But Emma didn't say a word. She stood real still with her hands pushed hard in her pockets.

"Miss Bloom says Laura's mother's here to help poor people, and that clinic's helping our town," I announced. I looked at Jesslyn, then back at my daddy.

"It's good that you and your mother gave up your summer for those in need, isn't it, girls?" he said. "Do you have family back in Ohio?" he asked Laura.

"Just my grandma and grandpa," she answered. She kept her eyes on the napkin in her lap. "They're worried," she said quietly. "They didn't want us to come."

I put down my fork and stopped chewing. "Why not?"

Jesslyn ignored me and looked right at Laura. "Have you been reading about the civil rights workers in the paper?"

"My mother says we mustn't read the newspapers here," Laura said. "They've been making up hateful things about her friends causing trouble."

"I've read letters to the editor of the *Hanging Moss*

Tribune saying they should stay up North where they belong," Jesslyn said. "Not everybody agrees with the newspaper, though."

"Who writes letters like that?" I asked. "Frankie's daddy's not too happy about what's going on. You reckon he writes to the newspaper?"

"A lot of folks are pleased about the Freedom Clinic your mama's running," Daddy said. "You'll see. People will come around."

"Why would anybody not like a clinic that helps poor people?" I asked. Most I'd read in our newspaper was what was playing at the picture show. Sometimes Frankie would make fun of the paper's Society Page, silly stuff about parties and who's visiting in Hanging Moss. I'd never read letters about people from up North here to make trouble.

"You're too young to read letters to the newspaper editor, Glory." Jesslyn stuck her nose up in the air. She took a sip of her iced tea, then smiled with her lips closed. "When you're old enough, you'll realize what was going on here this summer."

"I *am* old enough. And it's not like you know everything. What are you doing to help those in need, like Daddy says?"

Jesslyn had stopped being nice and was back up on her high horse again. My big sister could be so aggravating! I wanted to kick her under the table, hard. But when I glanced over at Laura, she was looking back and forth from me to Jesslyn, and twisting her napkin in her lap with both hands.

Right then I decided to be nice to Jesslyn.

"I got an idea. Miss Bloom asked me and Laura to do a special story time when the library has their thank-you celebration after the Fourth of July." I smiled real big at Laura, then back at my sister. "Maybe you could help us, Jesslyn? Miss Bloom's inviting Laura's mama and her friends, too. All those Yankees, coming to our library!"

Daddy looked like he might be about to say something, then changed his mind. Jesslyn stopped her fork midway to her mouth. They got all quiet. Maybe what I said about the library worried them.

Just then Emma stepped into the dining room holding her red velvet cake, and Jesslyn looked up at the clock ticking away on the buffet. "May I be excused?" she asked. "I'm late for meeting Mary Louise at the library." She pushed her chair back from the table. "Nice to have you for supper, Laura," she said, and she smiled at my friend but not at me, of course.

When we'd finished our cake, Emma appeared at the table to brush crumbs off the linen tablecloth. "Thank you for the delicious dinner," Laura said after she'd eaten every last bite of her cake. Maybe my new friend had found something to like here in Hanging Moss after all.

When Daddy headed back to the living room, I folded my napkin and stood up. "We'll clear the plates," I told Emma.

"You girls go on outside. Frankie will be here to play before you know it." She stopped brushing crumbs and looked right at me. "You be careful of his brother, Glory. That boy has a bad mean streak about him." Then the swinging door creaked shut, and the bright white of Emma's uniform skirt disappeared into the kitchen.

Chapter Nine

A FIRECRACKER BLEW OFF HIS FINGER

*A*fter supper, Laura and me sat on the back steps listening to the crickets start up. You could about catch a lightning bug by holding your hand out. Before we knew it, we were slapping mosquitoes and I had to turn on the stoop light to see real good.

"My friend Frankie's coming by to play. But I think he's mad at me," I said, as if Laura cared. I looked up at the porch light shining on the backyard. "I just hope he shows up before it gets too dark to play Kick the Can."

Laura stared at me like I was talking Pig Latin. "Kick the Can?" She shook her head. "Do you ever play jacks with your friend?"

"Outside at night," I told her, "we play Kick the Can or baseball."

"I'm not allowed to play outside at night. I live in an apartment, in a city." Laura smiled. "Once, my grandfather took me to an Indians game. Just me and Grandpa. Back in Ohio."

I jumped off the step and showed Laura the spot where we'd worn down the grass for home plate. Then I pointed to the big pecan tree. "See that tree? That's first base. And the water faucet, that high one sticking up out of the ground back there? That's second." I ran from the pecan tree to the faucet and stopped to catch my breath. "Third base is the steps where you're sitting." I raced to tag the steps and slid home just as Frankie and J.T. showed up.

"Hey, Glory. What're you doing?" Frankie fiddled with the whistle hanging from the lanyard around his neck.

"I'm teaching my friend how we play baseball here in Hanging Moss." I dusted the dirt off my shorts. "This is Frankie," I said to Laura. "And that's his brother, J.T."

I pressed my lips hard so I wouldn't introduce J.T. with what I really thought of him—Frankie's fat, ugly brother.

J.T. looked at Laura's brown sandals. He said, "You plan to run far in them clodhoppers?" J.T.'s about two times as tall as Frankie and ten times as mean.

"I could play in my socks." Laura started unbuckling her sandals.

J.T. laughed a snorty sound out of his nose. "You're wearing socks? In the summer? Black socks? What's the matter with you, Yankee?"

"Mind your own business, J.T." I untied my red sneakers. "I'm playing barefooted, Laura. That's the easiest. How 'bout you, Frankie?"

J.T. jabbed his scary half finger at Frankie. "Remember what Daddy told you, little brother."

Laura was barefooted by now, just like me. She'd dropped her shoes and those dumb black socks in a pile and stood up, ready to play.

"You wanna bat, Frankie?" I asked. But Frankie hadn't budged. "What's the matter? Just 'cause your brother doesn't want to play, you're leaving?" He stood there looking at J.T. like maybe his brother had something halfway sensible to say for once.

J.T. leaned down and kicked at something on the ground. He nodded at Frankie and glanced toward the step where me and Laura had lined up our shoes. Then he stuffed his hand in his pocket and started to walk away. "Let's go." He stopped and turned, waiting with his eyes set hard on his brother. "You comin'?"

Frankie looked at me, then Laura. "I can't stay." He moved closer. "My brother'll tattle to Daddy that I was playing baseball with a Yankee," he said to me. He rubbed his arm at the place where J.T. usually whacked him every time he opened his mouth. "Or worse."

"Why're you always doing everything he tells you?" I asked. "J.T. is not your daddy." For the life of me, I don't know why Frankie worships the ground his big brother walks on.

"My little brother ain't supposed to play with no Yankees, here to cause trouble and mess up our town." J.T. narrowed his eyes at Laura. "Wish you'd go back to where you came from." Then he spit a gob in the dirt next to Laura's bare feet. She jumped back, trying to get away from J.T.'s spit and his ugly words. "You need to get out of Hanging Moss, go where you're wanted, if there *is* any such place," he said, before strutting off toward his house.

"J.T. Smith, you stay away from me and my friend!" I hollered out, clenching my fists tight. "Stay away from my house and don't ever come back!" I turned to Frankie. "Why does he have to act so ugly?"

Laura moved nearer to me, reaching out for my hand, like she hoped I could save her from J.T. and his spit. "What happened to his finger?" she whispered.

"Top of it got blown off by a firecracker, a cherry bomb, two Fourth of Julys ago," I told her. "You'd think his brain got blown off. J.T. is dumb as a box of rocks."

"I don't like the way he talks." Laura pulled me closer to the back door, farther from Frankie. "And his finger is scary."

"Sometimes he tries to scare off little kids," I said. "Tells them he has his bloody finger in his pants pocket."

"Even with half a finger, my brother can do anything he wants to," Frankie said. He was taking up for his brother now. Seemed to be forgetting the punches, all the yelling. "He's the star of the football team, just like my daddy was," he said, sticking his chest out.

"That's about all your brother knows how to do," I said. "Play football and act mean."

"Frankie. You coming or not?" J.T. hollered from halfway down the block.

"I gotta go." Frankie's chest dropped. He kicked once at home base, then headed off down the street.

"Yeah, follow your stupid brother on home. We don't want you playing with us anyhow," I yelled after Frankie. "And I hope J.T.'s other finger gets blown off."

I'd lost my hankering for baseball. Besides, it wasn't

any fun with just me and Laura. "Let's just forget play-ing at night."

Laura looked relieved.

We sat on the back steps for a few more minutes, watching fireflies light on our hands.

"It's dark. We'd better go out front to wait for your mama." I handed her sandals over and grabbed my sneakers.

"Let's meet at the the park tomorrow. We can play jacks together. Or talk about Nancy Drew books," Laura said. "Or the Beatles! I'll be there early."

Before the back door had hardly slammed behind us, already I was glad I wouldn't be waiting for Frankie at Fireman's Park to make our lanyards and candles and bead bracelets at ten o'clock sharp, like we'd been doing every Friday morning since summer began. Now, I had somebody new to be a friend to.

Chapter Ten

J.T. STINKS

*F*rankie was back early the next afternoon. "Glory, open up. Please." He kept up with his *tap-tap-tap*ping on our kitchen screen door, quiet like, while I sat at the table reading more of *The Secret in the Old Attic*. I wasn't ready to talk, much less tell Frankie I'd been at Fireman's Park all morning with Laura.

But it was hard to ignore somebody who'd been your best friend all your life. And pretty soon he barged in the back door.

His words came out all in a jumble. "I'm sorry about last night. Not staying to play with you and that girl. My brother's just plain mean. Daddy gets him all riled up, talking about what might happen if somebody better than him makes the football team. Daddy's mad about everything. Doesn't want me talking to somebody from up North. Or somebody who's nice to people from up there."

I folded my arms. "What are you doing at my house?"

"Don't know," he said, slouching down in the chair next to me. "I wish it was last summer."

Since he was here sitting at my kitchen table looking pitiful, and since I'd already read *The Secret in the Old Attic* twice before, I decided to be halfway nice. "Where're you going?" I asked him.

"J.T. says Coach is making everybody work out in shoulder pads, get in shape for real football practices next month. I'm going over there to watch him sweat."

"You may worship the ground your mean, ugly brother walks on, but I never want to lay eyes on him again as long as I live," I told Frankie, and I meant it. "I'll only go with you to watch Jesslyn make a fool out of herself at pep squad practice."

We rode our bikes fast to the field. Frankie leaned into the chain-link fence, watching his brother like he was God's gift to the Hanging Moss High School Hornets. I moved to where I could hear the pep squad leader with her megaphone calling out stuff like "Pivot left! About-face!" Jesslyn marched with her hands on her hips and her nose in the air and her long curly hair not moving an inch from the ton of hairspray she'd used this morning.

Watching football players sweat would be more fun. I headed back and ran into Jesslyn's mystery boy from the library, holding the hose over his head. Stinking to high heaven.

"Hey, Jesslyn's little sister." He wiped his hands on his gold-and-black Hornets T-shirt and took a big drink. "I'm Robbie," he said. "Robbie Fox."

"How'd you know who I am?" I asked.

"Seen you around," he said.

J.T. yelled out to Robbie, "You, pretty boy, ready to quit? Too hot for you, Elvis?"

Robbie turned his back to J.T. and started down the field. I hurried to keep up with him.

"Wait up. Why'd he call you Elvis?" I asked.

"Something stupid about my hair, I guess."

"Are you new in town?" I was running along the fence, trying to keep up with Robbie Fox.

"Just moved here. Living with my aunt."

"Who's your aunt anyhow?" I called out. "Are you my sister's boyfriend?"

"You ask too many questions. I gotta go." When Robbie took off across the field, I moseyed back to sprawl out under a scrawny tree. The clouds drifted by and I turned the shapes into shells and ice-cream cones, thinking about this boy Robbie. Why was he here living with his aunt?

Pretty soon Frankie plopped down in the grass next to me. "Who's that you were talking to?" he asked.

"Jesslyn's friend, Robbie."

"My brother says Robbie Fox thinks he's hot snot. He brags all the time." Frankie pulled up clumps of grass and tossed them at the fence. "About how many touchdowns he made at his other school."

"J.T. and the rest of the stupid team oughta be happy. The Hornets stink at football," I said. Frankie didn't have an answer to that. He had plenty of book smarts from his encyclopedias, just didn't know diddly-squat about football. I wiped the sweat off my face with the back of my arm and scooted closer to the skinny shade tree. "It's hot as Hades out here. Let's get our bathing suits and head to the pool later."

"It closed." Frankie announced this like the pool was something we didn't give a toe bone about. Might as well have been saying the Piggly Wiggly was closed.

"*What?* The Community Pool's really *closed*? Why didn't you tell me?"

"Don't have a cow, Glory." Frankie looked past me, over at the football players running around the field and the pep squad girls hollering cheers to empty bleachers. "You were so mad from last night, I didn't want to say anything," he said. "Daddy and the Town Council put a sign up this morning saying they're fixing the cracks."

"There *aren't* any *cracks*."

"Daddy's committee had a meeting. He told me and J.T. it's really to keep the colored people out." Frankie took off his glasses, started cleaning them on his shirt. His voice got quiet. "I'm not supposed to tell."

"Well, what're we gonna do about it? I'll have a sunstroke if I have to spend the rest of the summer with no pool. I'm not swimming in the Pee Pool where all the babies go wading."

"I don't know" was all Frankie said.

"It's not right for some stupid committee of old people to decide who swims in a pool and who doesn't. Why's it a secret anyhow? A secret from who?"

Frankie put his glasses back on and shrugged his shoulders at me. "A secret from people like you who'd get mad about it, I guess," he said.

"Well, it's worth getting mad about. And what about the Fourth of July picnic and parade?" I asked him. "What about my birthday party in eight more days? It'll open back up by then, I'm sure."

Frankie pulled up a few more chunks of grass. He didn't say anything for a minute or two. "I don't know, Glory. My brother says it's a good thing they don't let colored people and Yankees in there to swim," he said. "J.T. thinks coloreds and Yankees stink."

"You wanna know who stinks? J.T. stinks, that's who. He doesn't know anything. And your daddy doesn't run this town, does he?"

Frankie may have thought his daddy knew everything, but what he said about the pool didn't seem right. "I'm going to see for myself."

We walked our bikes to the sidewalk. Then we rode real slow down the block. Maybe if I didn't get there and read the sign, the pool wasn't closed. But there it was, tacked up on the locked front gate of the Hanging Moss Community Pool for all the world to see: *Closed for repairs until further notice. By order of the Hanging Moss Town Council.*

"You see anybody in there patching the cracks?" I pushed my fingers through the metal fence and peered inside. The water was glimmering and peaceful, not a ripple, not one clue that anything was wrong. I pressed my face up closer for a better look. "Is somebody fixing the broken part of the fence over by our mimosa tree?"

All Frankie said was "Nope."

"I want to rip that pool sign to a million pieces and climb over the fence and swim."

Really and truly, what I wanted was to scream real loud at Frankie's daddy. Maybe even at Frankie. Deep down inside, a small part of me wanted Laura and her mama to go on back to Ohio so the pool would open.

"It's not right. It might as well be the dead of winter in there, Frankie," I said. "Nobody's swimming. No lifeguard whistles. No radios blaring. Nothing like it used to be." I pushed my fingers harder through the fence.

Frankie just shook his head. "I told you so."

"I'm getting out of here." I rode my bike down the street fast. I leaned it next to the tallest tree shading the library sidewalk. I didn't look back once at Frankie.

Chapter Eleven

MISS B. SAYS HOGWASH!

I banged open the library's front door and charged in.

Miss Bloom sat at the big checkout desk. "Hello, Glory." She mouthed the words as she patted the chair next to her. I sank into the hard wooden seat and propped my head in my hand.

"I can assure you that won't be happening," she said into the phone. She straightened her back and spoke very slowly. One word at a time. Like maybe the person on the other end of that phone wasn't hearing her too good. "We will not" — she stopped to take a deep breath — "be removing" — another breath — "library chairs. Anyone who wants to use the Hanging Moss Free Public Library is welcome here. Unlike the Town Council's Pool Committee, I will never allow the library to close." Then Miss Bloom hung up the telephone with two fingers, so carefully I thought maybe it had cooties on it she didn't want to touch.

"Are you mad at somebody, Miss B.?" I asked her.

"That was one of my board members. They worry there's going to be trouble at the library. They are suggesting I remove all the chairs so anyone they think doesn't belong here won't be welcome to sit down." Miss Bloom fiddled with the box of paper clips on her desk. "Or they say to close it altogether. Over my dead body will the library close."

"The pool's closed," I told her. "Frankie's daddy claims it won't open in time for July Fourth, the picnic and parade."

"I've worried about that." She shook her head and sat back in her chair. "It's a shame."

"I might not go to the stupid celebration anyhow." I twisted my ponytail.

"Glory, you love the Fourth of July—it's your birthday." Miss Bloom peered over her cat's-eye glasses. "Besides, Laura is counting on sitting with you."

"The parade's the same stupid thing every year." I crossed my arms and slumped deeper into the chair. "A bunch of old men carrying flags. A parade queen with a fake crown. Mrs. Simpson and the Esthers in their muumuus and bathing caps covered with plastic flowers, perched up on the biggest float like they own the town." I looked at Miss Bloom. "What fun's a July Fourth celebration when it's blazing hot and there's no swimming pool? You think anybody'll remember it's my birthday? Not even Jesslyn! Even if I have a party, Frankie's daddy won't let him come. Everything's going wrong!" I stopped to catch my breath. "How can anybody think closing the pool's fair?"

"That's a lot of questions, honey." Miss Bloom pulled a big book off the shelf behind her and dusted it with her hankie, which was embroidered with cats. When she slipped her hankie back up her jacket sleeve, she set the book in front of me, real careful. "Look here. We have scrapbooks from every celebration," she said.

I pointed to a faded picture tacked down with little silver triangles. "Who's that funny-looking man?"

"Your friend Frankie's grandfather, when he was young. See there? He owned the first car in town and decorated it up for July Fourth." Miss Bloom turned the scrapbook's crumbly black pages.

"Stupid Frankie says his daddy won't let him play with me anymore because of Laura." I looked at the picture of his grandfather sitting in that old car. I thought about Frankie. And about Laura, and Jesslyn. How some friends seem born into your life and others just pop up when you need them. But shouldn't a sister be both kinds of friends? Jesslyn used to be both, but I was starting to wonder.

Now Miss Bloom turned to a picture of the swimming races from a long time ago. "What's wrong with our pool?" I asked. "You think it will open by July Fourth?"

"Some people are unhappy that it's closed. And probably just as many think it ought to stay that way," Miss Bloom said. "A few of our citizens would like to see our town shut down tight—even the library— or at least go back to the way it was in Frankie's grandfather's day," she said. "But that's not going to happen."

I reached under the desk to pet her cat, Bobbsey. I felt like climbing under there to curl up in the coolness next to Bobbsey. "There's nothing wrong with the pool, is there?"

"I don't think so, Glory. At least nothing that can be fixed with cement. Hanging Moss is all mixed up about a lot of things. We have to figure this out, work together. But if you're worried about the pool, maybe you can do something," she said.

"Oh, sure. Me, eleven years old, get people like Frankie's hateful daddy to open it and let everybody in town swim." I kicked at the desk in time to the cat purring.

"Gloriana, it's not just Frankie's father who counts. First of all, there's the law. Believe me, if the law says the Community Pool stays open, sooner or later it will be open."

"Yeah, well, I don't understand that. The law and all."

"Look here." Miss Bloom turned to a row of newspapers hanging on a rack of wooden rods. She opened the *Hanging Moss Tribune* to a page of letters. "See these?"

"Are those what people send to the editor of the paper? Daddy told us about those letters. I wanted to see them, but Jesslyn claims I'm too young to read them."

"Hogwash. You read whatever you want to. If you've a mind to, I do believe you could write a letter yourself." Miss Bloom handed me the newspaper.

I sat up straighter. I turned the paper toward me. *Dear Editor,* one started. *I am writing to express my displeasure at the way the Hanging Moss Town Council has responded to the recent upheavals in our community.*

That was sure a heap of words saying nothing. "Can I borrow some stationery, Miss Bloom?" I asked. "I can write a better letter than that."

Chapter Twelve

OLD LADY SIMPSON SLAMS
THE DOOR

I caught my breath from running down the street. I pushed open my front door. I raced through the house, making enough noise to get some attention.

Emma was outside hanging Daddy's shirts on the clothesline. "Calm down, Glory. What's the matter?"

I held up my letter with about a million words crossed out. "Guess what this is, Emma. I'm writing to the *Hanging Moss Tribune* newspaper. I'm telling the editor that somebody in this town needs to figure out what's wrong with our pool. And fix it."

Emma poked a clothespin at a shirt to hang it. She did the same thing with another, then another, till a line of stiff white shirts floated upside down in the sunshine. Finally, she picked up the laundry basket and looked at me.

"Gloriana, you sure you know what you're doing?"

I didn't stop to answer, just turned around and went looking for more paper. I found today's *Tribune*, a writing tablet, a pencil, and envelopes on Daddy's desk. I brought these to the kitchen table and spread them out. Emma came to sit with her sack of snap beans in her lap.

"I'm writing my own letter. Miss Bloom thinks I can." I opened up the tablet.

"What you got to say to that newspaper?" she asked, snapping green beans without even looking at the bowl.

"Plenty." I started to read.

Dear Editor,

Closing down our pool in the ~~middle~~ hottest time of the summer is the ~~dumbest~~ worst idea on earth. It stinks that you're closing our pool. ~~Please~~ open it ~~soon~~ now!

I looked up at Emma.

"Sounds like messing in something you don't know a thing about. You might want to tell Brother Joe this first," she said, snapping beans faster and faster.

"I'm not telling anybody. I don't want to be making any nosy church people mad, thinking he helped me. Or Jesslyn saying I don't write big enough words. And I sure don't want Frankie worrying I'm giving away any of his stupid secrets."

Emma stopped snapping beans and looked straight at me. "A fish that never opens his mouth won't get caught."

I put down my pencil. "What's that mean?"

"Means if you keep your mouth closed, you don't make trouble. Watch out you don't get us *all* in trouble."

"Don't worry, Emma. I know what I'm doing." I opened a clean sheet of paper and started over.

Dear Tribune Editor,

Do you know how hot it is in the summer? All the children of Hanging Moss want someplace to swim.

Words buzzed around my head like a mosquito that needed swatting. Emma shook her head slowly. "If you're bound and determined to write this letter, at least think hard about saying the right thing."

"I'm *trying*. Shoot. This letter writing is harder than

I thought." I ripped my paper to shreds and stomped out of the kitchen. Emma followed me into the dining room.

"Come back here, Glory. Sit down." She patted the back of the high wooden chair. She handed me the paper and pencil. "Take this and begin again. Always a good idea to start with saying something nice. Leave your vinegar till the end." She smiled and put her hand over mine, and I remembered our hands together, like Daddy's statue. I took a deep breath.

"I might need some help saying *It stinks that our pool closed* in a nicer way."

"Try thinking about what really matters to you about your pool," Emma said. "And not just your birthday party. You can do this." She laughed when I wrinkled my nose up at her, then she disappeared into the kitchen.

I chewed on the pencil. Thought some more. Crossed parts out. Tore up the whole thing and started over. I looked it over one last time.

"Emma, come here please," I called out. "I'm ready!"

When she finished reading, Emma shook her head and said quietly, "What have you done *now*, Glory? What *have* you done?"

"I meant every word of it," I said. "Every single word." I jerked my letter away from her.

"Then I guess I'm proud of you, baby, even if you do get us all in a whole lot of trouble."

I felt my shoulders loosen for the first time all day.

I sealed up the envelope. I memorized the address I'd written on the outside in my best script. Then I put the letter in my back pocket, real careful, and headed across to 233 East Main Street. I looked in the big glass window with *Hanging Moss Tribune* painted in fancy letters across the front. Still open.

Wait a dang minute! Was that my neighbor Mrs. Simpson with her green-tinged hair all done up in a fat bun, inside the *Tribune*'s office, typing away at a desk right by the door? What was *she* doing here?

I tapped on the window, smiled, and waved. Mrs. Simpson glanced up, paying me as much attention as she does when she's playing the piano at Daddy's church. I took a deep breath to stop my heart from pounding. Then I marched right in.

"Hello, Mrs. Simpson," I said, polite as a preacher's kid. The air conditioner in the window was making such a racket I wasn't sure she'd heard me. "Hello, Mrs. Simpson," I said again, shivering in the cold office.

"Gloriana Hemphill. What brings you to the *Tribune*?" She smiled in that grown-up way that means people don't care about hearing the answer.

"A letter. I have a letter to the newspaper editor." I reached in my pocket and handed it across the desk. My heart was pounding. I tried to picture Mrs. Simpson in her big flowered bathing suit with the skirt billowing out, swimming with those Esthers at the Community Pool instead of sitting behind that newspaper desk looking like a hawk ready to pounce on a baby bird.

"What a sweet thing to do." She hardly glanced up from her typewriter. "What's your little letter about, dearie?"

"It's about the pool," I said. "I don't think it's right to close it. Or to keep people out just because they aren't white."

"Oh." Mrs. Simpson's mouth *made* the letter O when she spoke. "I'll see that the editor gets this." Mrs. Simpson looked like she'd just smelled rotten eggs. She held my letter by one corner and dropped it in her desk drawer. I peered over her desk just as she banged the drawer shut.

"When will my letter be in the paper?" I asked.

"As soon as there's room on the Letters to the Editor

page. And, of course, we have to check for grammatical mistakes. And be sure the writer composed the letter him- or herself." Mrs. Simpson moved toward the front door. "I hope Brother Joe is aware of your letter writing," she said, holding the door open.

"Yes, he is," I lied. When I stepped outside, a blast of heat made me want to sink down on the sidewalk to catch my breath. But I kept moving. "And for your information I composed that letter myself," I yelled into the hot, empty air. "Every single word!"

But Mrs. Simpson slammed the door and turned the sign to *Closed*, trapping the cold inside.

Chapter Thirteen

JESSLYN'S BIG FAT LIE

I ran all the way to my front steps without stopping, and plunked onto the porch swing. My head was spinning thinking about mean Old Lady Simpson, but I wasn't gonna tell what I'd done. I kicked off my sneakers to push the swing back and forth with my bare feet, catching my breath under the ceiling fan.

Pretty soon, here came Jesslyn gliding up the sidewalk. She didn't say a single thing, just floated up the stairs to our room. I followed her and opened my newest Nancy Drew book to chapter eleven, all the time thinking about the letter I'd just delivered to Mrs. Simpson.

Jesslyn leaned across her bed and reached under it. Was that her shoe box she was after? I was hopeful.

"Wanna play Junk Poker?" I asked. But she had

already pushed the box back under her bed and was heading down the stairs.

"I told you, that's a baby game," she called back. "I cleaned out my box."

But I'd seen Jesslyn slip something inside. As soon as she was gone, I peeked down the hall to be sure she wasn't coming back. I shut our bedroom door, then sneaked out her Junk Poker shoe box. I held my breath, hoping my big sister hadn't forgotten something. I untied her box's ribbon, ignoring the *Keep Out* and *Private, This Means You* notes taped to the top.

Yep. She'd dumped her old junk out all right. But she'd saved a library card with Robert Aaron Fox's name on it—big as life and stamped today, June 26, 1964.

My heart was beating like nobody's business when I put Robbie's library card back and quickly shoved the shoe box under the bed. I marched downstairs, sat myself on the sofa, and pretended to read Jesslyn's movie magazine. No one seemed to notice me.

"I'll be back before dark," Jesslyn was saying to our daddy. "Mary Louise wants me to go to Memphis to shop tomorrow. Her cousin's driving us."

"Can't you find what you need here in town? The idea of you going off to Memphis." His voice drifted off, and he stared out the window across to the church. Looked to me like he wished he was someplace else. Someplace he could turn to the Good Book for advice and not worry about his daughter wanting to spend tomorrow shopping for fire batons, bathing suits, and party favors in Memphis, Tennessee.

"Can I go with you?" I asked.

"You're not invited, Glory," Jesslyn said, clamping her teeth together.

"I've never been anywhere. I need a new bathing suit, too. Can't I come?" I asked.

"Glory, *you* may not go to Memphis," our daddy said. "That's that." Then he looked hard and long at Jesslyn. "And you, young lady, I'll think about letting you go if you'll be home before dark."

"Yes, sir." Jesslyn smiled at Daddy, then gave me one of her looks.

But I wasn't giving up that easy. "If you let me go, Jesslyn and Mary Louise could help me get things for my birthday party. In case the pool opens back up. You know, it *is* my birthday on July Fourth, eight days away. In case y'all have forgotten."

Nobody paid a bit of attention to me.

Jesslyn was smiling sweetly at Daddy.

"We'll be careful. And we'll be back before dark. Memphis is only an hour away. Can I *please* go with Mary Louise? Her cousin is a very good driver."

And since I was the only living soul who knew a thing about a new boy in town asking Jesslyn to ride someplace all by herself in his car with him, our daddy thought for only a minute longer before he said yes.

Chapter Fourteen

TRYING TO BREATHE UNDER
A BLANKET

By eleven o'clock the next day, Jesslyn had been up and down the stairs all morning, turning this way and that at the front hall mirror, ignoring me. I was in the kitchen with Emma where it felt like a zillion degrees. Too hot to be cooking turnip greens and frying pork chops, but that's what Emma did in the middle of most every day. I waited for her to put the corn bread in the oven and sit with me.

"Guess what, Emma. I delivered our letter to the newspaper." I smiled and reached for her hand.

"Don't be calling that *our* letter." She pulled her hand back and picked up a stack of napkins to fold. "Just 'cause I helped you with a few words." She shook her head.

"I sure hope you don't get your daddy in trouble. Now this mess with Jesslyn going to Memphis. Shopping, humph." Emma stood up and started banging pots and pans and singing about gathering at the river, a sure sign she suspected something.

"Is Daddy coming home to eat with us?" I asked.

"Brother Joe's over at the church, been there since after breakfast working on his sermon. I suspect he won't come back for his usual noontime meal and nap today."

"You aren't gonna tell him about my letter, are you?"

"I'm not mentioning that letter to anybody," Emma said. "But I'm worried about your sister. She needs to be careful running all over God's green earth like that. Especially now, this summer, with people all riled up about *outsiders* and Northerners and pools closing."

I shut up about my letter and pretty soon, here came Jesslyn, dressed for her fake shopping trip. Emma pointed her wooden spoon at Jesslyn's skirt. "You going out of the house in that?"

"It's the style and I like it." Jesslyn spread a huge napkin over her new plaid skirt and picked at a piece of hot corn bread. I sat at the other end of the kitchen table, pretending to read every single word on page forty-six of *The Secret in the Old Attic*.

Emma said, "That style is almost hiked up to your underpants for the whole world to see—you need to find something else to wear."

Jesslyn didn't talk back to Emma, but she didn't go upstairs and change, either.

"Watch yourself today is all I'm saying. Memphis is a big place." Emma started washing and drying her glass measuring cups. She was pressing on them so hard, I thought they'd break.

Jesslyn smiled, holding her lips together. "Don't worry. I'm old enough to take care of myself. Besides, I'll be back before dark." She fiddled with the bracelet she'd just clasped around her wrist, then flipped it toward me like she knew how much I'd love my own silver bracelet filled with little charms. After she set her dish and iced tea glass in the sink, she dabbed at her bright lipstick. Then she shut the front door and half skipped down the sidewalk toward wherever it was she claimed she was going.

Emma called after Jesslyn, "Watch yourself, girly!"

But Jesslyn was long gone.

"Something not right with this so-called shopping

trip," Emma said. "That child's been acting strange lately."

It wasn't easy to get anything past Emma. That's why the lie I was about to tell came out of my mouth slowly, carefully.

"Emma, I forgot to tell you. Miss Bloom asked me and Laura to help with the little kids' story program over at the library," I said. "All afternoon."

Emma put her hand on my shoulder to stop me from running off the way Jesslyn had just done. She was looking at me hard. She must've still been thinking about Jesslyn — and Jesslyn's skirt.

"Just a minute, young lady. *All* afternoon?"

When I looked right back at Emma, I didn't blink. It was hard to lie and not blink.

"Miss Bloom needs me. Plus, I have to drop my book off." I took a deep breath and told my heart to stop beating so fast. I shook loose from Emma's hand. She'd never come looking for me at the library. Come to think of it, Emma had never set foot in our library.

"Gotta go." The screen door slammed behind me. "Sorry about the door," I yelled back.

Whew. I'd escaped without Emma figuring out I was not going to be spending the day at the library.

I looked up and down Church Street. No Jesslyn. Then I caught a glimpse of a red plaid skirt sashaying down the shady side street by the library. Jesslyn was prissing like she owned the world. I ducked behind a wide pecan tree and watched a gold Plymouth station wagon stop in front of her. A black wavy ducktail haircut and an arm hanging out the window told me what I already suspected.

Jesslyn was running off with Robbie Fox!

He opened the car door, big as you please. But something must've changed his mind because the next thing I knew they'd disappeared into the Piggly Wiggly grocery store across the street. I raced to that station wagon and peered in the back window. A picnic cooler, a blanket, an old football jersey, and the spare tire were inside.

When I heard Jesslyn back on the sidewalk, yakking nonstop, I didn't have but a minute to decide.

I jumped in the wayback of the station wagon to hide under the blanket. Wherever we were going, I hoped it didn't take long. This was the scratchiest blanket ever. And I couldn't hardly breathe.

Chapter Fifteen

HOT, SQUISHED, ITCHING

We were riding fast. The radio blasted that new Elvis song Jesslyn had played a zillion times on her record player, something about suspicion.

I kept quiet and rested my sweaty forehead against the picnic cooler.

I heard Robbie say, "Glad you thought of getting something cold to drink for the ride. I brought my camera, to take your picture in front of the house."

But I kept still, barely breathing.

"I saw you practicing football," Jesslyn said after a while. "Everybody's saying you were the star back where you moved from. Why'd you leave?"

"It's complicated," he said. "And private. Promise you won't tell?"

I got a worried feeling in the pit of my stomach like I'd eaten something rotten. Then somebody must have clicked the radio off because all I heard was the sound of wind whooshing through the windows and them shaking the ice in their Cokes.

I managed to hear Jesslyn say, "I'm good at secrets. Preachers' kids hear a lot of stuff. Daddy has taught us not to gossip." Yeah, well, he might have taught Jesslyn, but I still had work to do on that lesson.

At first, Robbie didn't answer. I listened hard into the whooshing wind and rattly Coke ice. Then Robbie's words tumbled out, loud enough for me to hear. "I promised my aunt I wouldn't tell this. She doesn't want everybody sticking their noses in our family's business."

Robbie got quiet again. Finally he said, "If I hadn't come to live in Hanging Moss . . ." Robbie struggled with his voice, then managed, ". . . I might be in jail."

Jail?

Jesslyn and me were riding in a car to Kingdom Come with a jailbird?

I put my hand over my mouth to keep it from yelping. Emma would have our heads—and our tails—on a platter!

For the first time ever, Jesslyn was speechless.

She was probably thinking about Emma's wooden spoon coming in for a smack to the back of her *It's the style* skirt!

Quietly Robbie said, "I got in trouble back in North Carolina. It was in the newspapers."

"What kind of trouble?" Jesslyn asked carefully.

"There was this dime store with a place to eat inside. Just stools and a counter. Good hot dogs and ice cream. I saw a boy there. A colored friend named Henry. His daddy worked on my granddaddy's farm. Sometimes we'd throw the ball around, act like we were scoring. Henry was always nice to me. Our schools were getting ready to join up next year—our town wasn't really big enough to have a school for white students and a school for Negro ones. We would've ended up on the same football team."

I kept holding my breath.

"Henry was sitting there waiting to order something. One of his friends was reading a book. They were talking quietly, not doing anything bad. 'Cept, in our town, colored people aren't supposed to eat where white people eat."

I was all ears now. Robbie could have been describing Hanging Moss—same thing for us. Colored people and white people are kept separate at pools, schools, restaurants—even the town library.

"What did you do?" Jesslyn asked.

"The waitress yelled at them to leave. So I found a stool next to Henry. I sat down to order. I didn't like that waitress hollering at Henry and his friends to get up. So I told her so. The police came. Pulled us out to the street. Of course, somebody called the newspaper."

Well, I'll be. If Jesslyn or me did that at the Five and Dime lunch counter downtown, Mrs. Simpson and her newspaper people would be there faster than you could say hot dog with mustard. I can't imagine what Daddy would do if my picture ended up on the front page of the *Hanging Moss Tribune*.

"I bet that was scary," Jesslyn said.

"I'm not sorry I did it. It *was* scary, though. The police hauled us off to jail. I stayed there till my step-daddy came that evening. I'd never done anything bad before, so they let me go with a warning. After that, Mama sent me here to my aunt's. Said she needed some time away from me. Claimed she couldn't hold her head up around town."

Now my heart was beating faster than fast. I wondered if Robbie was going the speed limit. My insides were *zooming*.

Jesslyn said, "Maybe your mama will change her mind and let you come home?"

"Yeah, well, I like it here now," Robbie said. "I'm gonna stay, especially if I make the football team."

"You'll make the team," Jesslyn said. "You're good."

The ice rattling had stopped and the wind had died down some. I could practically hear Jesslyn batting her eyes.

"Please don't tell anybody what happened in North Carolina. Word gets out I'm a troublemaker? My aunt might send me back. I don't want the team to know, either."

I shut my eyes tight, clinched my fists together, and willed myself not to push that scratchy blanket back, sit up, and say that Jesslyn wouldn't tell a single soul 'cause she's good at keeping secrets, and good at telling lies. *I* was bad at keeping secrets—and real bad at lying, especially to Emma.

The car radio came back on and all I could hear was Elvis singing. The picnic cooler bounced next to me while I thought about having a Dr Pepper with Jesslyn and Robbie soon, me pretending like I hadn't heard that bad thing about Robbie and his friend Henry.

The station wagon slowed, then stopped. We were

parked someplace. Jesslyn reached over to the backseat for the camera about the time Robbie opened the way-back door for the cooler. There was no more hiding. Both of them saw me at once.

Jesslyn looked like she'd seen a ghost. "*Glory?* What are you doing? How'd you get back there?" She stormed out, slammed her car door, and stood next to Robbie. She reached over and grabbed my wrist, squeezed it so hard she could've given me a rope burn. I twisted away and shut my mouth up tight. My sister was mad as a hornet. "Have you been spying on us?"

"I wanted to see where y'all were going. That's all." I glared at my sister. "I double-dog dare you to fuss at me! You're not supposed to be here any more than I am. Isn't shopping in Memphis with Mary Louise fun?"

When I looked over at Robbie, he had his jaw clenched tight.

"Stay in this station wagon," Jesslyn hissed. "And *stay quiet.*"

I was all squished up next to the drink cooler.

"You're not the boss of me." There was a little house right next to where we were parked. "Where *are* we? What's that broken-down shack over there?"

"You'll never know," Jesslyn said. "You aren't budging out of the car."

Robbie must've taken some pity on me. "Let her out. It's hot back there."

"She can burn up for all I care. She's not coming with us." Jesslyn's voice was full of meanness. "And you'd better not tell. I mean it, Glory."

Robbie grabbed the cooler and followed Jesslyn up the cracked sidewalk. She leaned over, pulled up a handful of grass from beside a front step of that little house by the road, and stuffed the grass in her back pocket.

I sat in the station wagon, hot, squished, itching to get out.

"I'm coming whether you like it or not," I hollered out. Even if it was just some falling-down house on a street in the middle of nowhere, I wanted to see what they were doing. When I stepped on the porch steps, it felt like the whole house would cave in. "Where are we?"

"Not far from Hanging Moss, if you knew anything at all. This is Tupelo. Elvis lived here when he was a little boy." Jesslyn hugged herself like this was as good as meeting Elvis himself. I mean, this place was downright pitiful, and Jesslyn was acting like it was a palace.

I looked around. "If this was Elvis's house, you'd

think it'd be a little fancier. Nothing but dead bushes and a cracked window."

"What'd you expect, big iron gates? You don't know anything, Glory."

Robbie pushed back his black hair that was combed just like Elvis's in the picture Jesslyn kept taped to the mirror in our room. "Elvis wasn't rich when he lived here. Not that many people know about this house," Robbie said. He spit on his shirttail, wiped circles in the dust of a front windowpane. "Hey, you gotta see this."

Jesslyn peered through the dirty window. "I dare you to get me some of that wallpaper." She batted her eyes like Robbie was the real Elvis passing out autographs.

"I'm going around back to break in." He jumped off the low porch and disappeared.

Jesslyn pulled me down to the front steps. "Don't move," she said. She followed Robbie around the corner of the house.

I rubbed my hand across the splinters on the steps, picturing Elvis being a little boy crawling around on this very porch. Not a breath of air moved, and the sun was so hot I got to wondering what in tarnation Jesslyn and Robbie were doing behind the house. Nancy Drew wouldn't just wait here. She'd be looking for clues.

Where were they? I spotted an open window! I peeked in just in time to see Robbie peel off a piece of wallpaper and hand it to Jesslyn like it was a diamond ring. I could hear them talking plain as day.

"If we hold the camera back, both of us can be in the picture." Then I saw a flashbulb pop light and heard Jesslyn giggling.

I waited in the dirt and dried-up grass and thought about all those nights last summer when we stayed up late talking about how yucky boys were. Now Jesslyn had disappeared with Robbie into the cool shadows of Elvis's living room and I didn't hear talking anymore. Pretty soon they climbed back out the open window, acting all moony-eyed.

That's when Jesslyn saw me sitting there.

"I told you to wait on the front porch." She looked right into my eyes. She was squinting hard.

"I wanna see inside, too," I told her. "You never used to mind if I went places with you."

"I mind now."

The heck with Jesslyn! I climbed right through the window of Elvis's house.

Whew. It smelled like the inside of Frankie's hamster cage. I got out fast and hurried around to the front porch. "Stinks to high heaven in there. When's the picnic?" I asked.

Robbie handed me a drink and a cookie. I dangled my legs off the porch in the sweltering heat while they giggled and whispered. This porch-sitting was getting boring.

"It'll be getting dark soon," I said. "Emma might notice we're gone."

We packed up Robbie's station wagon. Before we left, I reached down and stole me some of Elvis's grass, too. Then I slipped in the backseat, right behind Jesslyn.

"This is pretty. Thank you." Jesslyn curled her fingers around the piece of green-flowered wallpaper. She put her head back on the seat and looked at Robbie. "I had fun today," she said.

I squeezed my knees up close to my face and smiled, thinking about Elvis and that ugly wallpaper. I stopped smiling when I thought about Robbie and what he said about jail.

"We need to hurry. It's getting dark," I said.

Right about now, all I wanted was to get home to Emma, safe and sound.

Chapter Sixteen

ALMOST DARK

*T*hat evening, by the time Robbie's headlights hit the *Welcome to Hanging Moss, Mississippi, Population 8,003* sign out on the highway, the sun was sinking behind the trees and the sky was a million colors of orange. We were almost home. I leaned against Robbie's backseat, thinking about the day. And what Emma would say if she found out Jesslyn and I were joyriding with Robbie, the North Carolina jailbird.

Jesslyn hollered so loud it woke me out of my day-dreaming. She leaned over to shake my knee. "Glory, is somebody following us?"

I turned around. "Oh, no," I said. "The car's got a big red light on the top."

"Uh-oh," Robbie said, before he pulled in next to a

small store advertising corn, tomatoes, and green beans.

"It's a policeman." I was taking in big gulps of air. I could hardly talk. "He's getting out of his car."

Jesslyn was whispering, "He's writing down our license plate number. Wonder if he's been following us all along?"

Robbie looked in his rearview mirror.

When the policeman tapped on our window, Jesslyn and I nearly jumped out of our skin. "I need your driver's license, son," he said to Robbie. "Get out of the car and turn around."

"Yes, sir." Robbie stepped outside. I scootched to the edge of my seat and leaned my head toward Jesslyn. Robbie reached into his back pocket to hand over his wallet.

"You're from North Carolina?" The policeman looked hard at Robbie's license. "What brings you down here?"

While Robbie explained about how he was here staying with his aunt for the summer, wanting to play football come September, my heart was pounding so hard I could hardly hear.

I wanted to be home where I belonged.

The policeman said, "There's people from out of

state down here stirring up trouble. You wouldn't be one of them, would you?"

"No, sir," Robbie said politely.

"Get back in your car. Drive straight on home. It's not safe to be out after dark tonight." Just when I didn't think this evening could get any worse, the policeman's hand brushed across his gun and he shined his flashlight in my eyes, then Jesslyn's. "You girls visiting from North Carolina, too?" he asked.

"Yes, sir," Jesslyn answered. And I was almost glad to hear her lie because lying to a policeman wasn't nearly as bad as what Emma and our daddy would've done if he'd dragged us home in his big car with that bright red light shining for all the world to see.

Then the policeman looked hard at me and Jesslyn. "You're sure you're not from around here?"

"No, sir," Jesslyn's voice squeaked out.

"You look kind of familiar." The policeman shined his flashlight around the backseat again.

Jesslyn didn't answer the policeman. Neither did I.

Pretty soon, he nodded at Robbie. "Son, you get these girls home. It's too late to be out on the highway. Whoever their daddy is, he'll be worrying."

Chapter Seventeen

CROSS MY HEART

When Robbie's car started up again, I was *shaking*. My fingernails dug into the backseat.

"You think that policeman's gonna get us in trouble somehow?" I finally asked. "Daddy will skin us alive if he finds out you're not shopping with Mary Louise and that we got stopped by the police." I dug my fingernails even deeper. "Once Daddy is done with us, it'll be Emma's turn to skin our hides."

"We didn't do anything wrong," Robbie answered.

"If you don't count Jesslyn lying to a policeman," I said.

We were back in town now. Robbie stopped the car in front of our house.

"Not here! Y'all better let me out by the library,"

I told him. "I'll walk home." The last thing I needed was for Emma to see me getting out of Robbie's car.

"You know, Glory," Jesslyn said, without even turning around to look at me, "you shouldn't go sneaking into people's business. Don't tell anything about today. Anything you saw. Or anything you heard."

"I didn't hear anything." I was gonna try real hard to keep Robbie's secret. Not like the time I blabbed to Emma that Jesslyn had broken our mama's china cat statue when I'd promised I wouldn't tell. Or when I let it slip to Frankie that Emma had sewed lace to Jesslyn's underpants for pep squad tryouts. Nope, not like that. This time I was keeping a real secret.

As long as I lived, I'd never tell this story. *If* I lived long enough to stand a shakedown by Emma or Daddy.

Robbie let me out around the corner from the library. "Glory, I'll be back at the house soon after you get there," Jesslyn said.

When I got home, Emma was waiting on the front porch. "You been at the library all this time?"

"Yessum."

"Get in here, Glory. Where's Jesslyn? She promised she'd be back before dark."

"It's not quite dark yet. I don't know where she is." I kept my eyes on the grass.

"Brother Joe's got a meeting at the church. He's due back any time now. When he finds out Jesslyn's not here —" Emma's voice stopped. "I never liked the idea of that child going off to Memphis shopping. When do you reckon your sister's getting home?"

"Don't know, don't care." I caught myself before another word popped out of my mouth. Jesslyn might get in trouble — but I wouldn't be the one telling on her. I walked into the kitchen like it was any other night of the summer. I sat at the table, eating a stick of Emma's warm corn bread. I turned the pages of Jesslyn's magazine and looked at the movie star Sandra Dee, with not one single solitary blond hair where it didn't belong. I focused my mind on how she'd have to sleep on brush rollers all night long to get that flipped-up hairdo.

When Emma walked in, she set down a plate of fudge big enough to feed half of Hanging Moss. I closed the magazine. "Can I have a piece?"

She handed me a tiny bite and covered it up. "I'm taking this home to my company," she said.

"Who's your company? Must be a heap of people to eat all that candy."

"Just visitors," she said.

Emma didn't ever have visitors. I'd been to her house over on the other side of town. There wasn't room for anybody but Emma. I looked at the big plate wrapped in tinfoil. "Who are they?"

"I got four or five folks sleeping on my sofa and in the back room."

"Who?" I asked again.

Emma sat at the kitchen table like she was plum worn out. She pulled her chair close to me. "Young folks from up north, like your friend Laura's mother. Your daddy knows," she said. "Some white people have fired maids for keeping civil rights workers, Freedom Workers, at their houses. But Brother Joe don't mind."

"Laura's mother's a Freedom Worker. Least that's what Frankie called her. He says it like freedom's something bad." I picked at a scab on my arm. I couldn't look at Emma. "Wonder if they'll try to get the pool opened up. Frankie says it's closed because of all the Yankees like Laura in town."

"Civil rights people here got a heap of things need doing besides that pool. Important things, like helping us figure out how to vote, teaching children to read," Emma said. "It's good you and Laura are friends.

I suspect she's lonely sitting at the library, what with her mama gone over to the new clinic."

"Frankie's mad about me being friends with Laura. His daddy says for him not to play with me." I looked right at Emma and took a deep breath. "And now the pool's closed," I said. "And you've got Yankees visiting. Lots of stuff is happening here, Emma."

Emma took my hand and held it up next to hers.

"Praying hands," I whispered.

"Praying hands. We got a lot to pray over, baby." She pushed herself up from the table, finished wrapping up the fudge to take home.

I went to the porch to think. Fireflies blinked on and off in the front yard, and the crickets chirped so loud it was hard to get my thoughts straight. Maybe I could just write another letter to that newspaper. Say how mean it was for a policeman to accuse any old boy out just riding on the highway of causing trouble. My daddy wouldn't need to know who wrote it. None of his church people would ever find out. A whole lot of those letters didn't have names signed to them. I could be *Anonymous* like they were.

When I peered down the sidewalk, Emma was waiting for her friend Mr. Miles's Liberty taxicab that picked her up some nights. I looked again, and finally, here came Jesslyn holding her sandals in one hand, fanning herself with a magazine with the other.

"Jesslyn's home!" I started down to meet her. "Did you have fun in Memphis with Mary Louise?" I yelled.

Emma mumbled something about Jesslyn not having the brains the good Lord gave a flea. Then she juggled the tinfoil-wrapped fudge and her giant pocketbook and eased herself into the backseat of the taxi. Lucky for Jesslyn, they drove off before Emma had a chance to ask anything about the so-called trip to Memphis.

Pretty soon, our daddy crossed the street and stood on the front porch. When we followed him inside, he carefully lined up his sermon and his Bible on the front hall table. "You and Mary Louise get what you needed?" he asked. "The fire baton and all?"

"We had fun, but I didn't buy anything 'cept some new magazines." She held up her movie magazine, which I knew she'd had all summer. "I'm tired, Daddy. Think I'll go upstairs to bed." Jesslyn gave me a *keep your mouth shut* look, and so I did. She walked in the kitchen, poured some iced tea, and took her glass upstairs. She pulled the hall phone into the bathroom and shut the door tight, with the extra-long cord squished under-neath the door.

I sat on my bed, real quiet so I could hear her.

Jesslyn was whispering. "We took a drive to Elvis's house in Tupelo—and got stopped by the police on the way home."

It had to be Mary Louise on the phone. I lay down on my bed and opened *The Witch Tree Symbol*. When Jesslyn stopped talking, I marked my place with a book-mark made out of a magnolia leaf I'd pressed in Bible School. Jesslyn waltzed into our room wearing pink pajamas and a goony, dreamy look. "Wanna play cards?" she asked.

I couldn't believe it.

"Sure. Junk Poker?" I grabbed for my box.

"Not that silly game," Jesslyn said. "Besides, Daddy doesn't like us betting on card games."

I didn't mention how he wouldn't like a lot of stuff she'd been up to lately.

"So what's in your shoe box you keep tied up under your bed if it's not junk for poker?"

"Nothing."

Since I'd looked inside that box, I knew what was in there. Soon she'd add the picture of her and Robbie at

Elvis's house and the scrap of green-flowered wallpaper.

"Let's play Gin Rummy," Jesslyn said.

I shuffled and dealt us each ten cards, then turned the next one over. "I wish we played together more, like we did last summer."

"Last summer was a long time ago, Glory." Jesslyn picked up a card.

I was quiet for a minute, thinking of what to say next. "I had fun in Tupelo with you and Robbie. Except for the last part. That was scary."

"Remember, you can't tell Daddy," Jesslyn said. "You can't tell where we went. You can't tell about the policeman. And you *especially* can't tell anybody anything you heard Robbie say."

"I didn't hear a thing."

I picked up the king of hearts and slapped it on the stack.

Jesslyn turned over her last card and shook her head. "I won. Again. You're not that great at cards, you know."

"Well, maybe if somebody played with me more," I started to say, but Jesslyn wasn't listening.

"Cut the light off."

I made the room dark, pulled back my bedspread, and crawled under the covers. The air conditioner was so loud I could barely hear Jesslyn's voice across the room.

"Glory, remember," she whispered, half asleep. "It's a secret."

In the dark, over my own pink pajamas, I crossed my heart. Then just to be sure, before falling asleep, I crossed my heart again.

Chapter Eighteen

THE STORM ON SUNDAY

The next day, on Sunday morning, Jesslyn and I stared out the window at little rivers of rain turning our backyard home plate into a wading pool. "We should head over to the church soon," Jesslyn said, as if I didn't know. "We can't be late."

In addition to saving souls over at First Fellowship, Daddy's job was turning on lights and ceiling fans. Shutting windows tight against the rain or opening them wide to let the Good Lord's sunshine in. Our job was to get ourselves to Junior Choir practice ten minutes before Mrs. Simpson played the first hymn. Days like this I wished my daddy was a veterinarian or a taxicab driver—anything but a preacher.

I shut my eyes, wishing I could pull Emma's quilt off

the bed in Mama's sewing room, cover up on the sofa next to the window, and read Nancy Drew to my heart's content.

"You think the rain will stop by the time we get to church?" I asked. Before Jesslyn could answer, somebody started *bam*ming hard on the front door.

"Glory, let me in! Hurry!"

Frankie's hair was plastered down from the rain. His glasses were fogged over. He was dripping puddles of water.

"Hold your horses, Frankie." I stepped back from the door. "What are you doing here?"

He held up what was left of a soggy sheet of paper. "This was in our mailbox. For my daddy from the Pool Committee. The pool's opening! Anybody can come."

Jesslyn led Frankie into the kitchen. When she smoothed the notice out on the table, it started to rip. The ink was blurred. But there it was, in black and white: *Pool Opening for July Fourth.*

"You reckon this means I can have my birthday there? And you and Laura and everybody can come? I won't believe it till I see the sign with my very own eyes," I said. "Let's go."

"Have you looked outside?" Jesslyn asked. "Nobody

goes to a swimming pool, open or closed, in this weather."

I didn't care. I wanted to be sure that *Pool Closed* sign was down.

"Frankie, get the umbrella, the big green one in the hall closet." I gave him the hairy eyeball. He'd better follow me quick.

"We're supposed to be at church before eleven. Daddy'll kill us if we show up drenching wet and late," Jesslyn said.

"Well, if you want to worry about being late to church the first time in our entire lives, head on upstairs and get your Sunday clothes on, Miss Priss," I told her, opening the umbrella. "Me and Frankie are going to the pool."

It didn't take long before Jesslyn was kicking off her shoes and grabbing another umbrella. I was smiling big as all get-out.

Purple clouds filled up the sky as she and I hiked up our shorts and waded barefoot through the warm muddy water.

"You should have kept your shoes on." Frankie stepped around a wide brown puddle. "This stuff is full of germs. All the dead bugs and dog doo in the street.

My science book says rainwater's polluted. Not much different from the baby pool down at Fireman's Park, if you ask me."

Not that we'd sloshed around barefooted in the Pee Pool with the babies lately.

"Don't be such a sissy. It's just mud and rainwater," Jesslyn said. "You need to get your nose out of those science books, Frankie." Once she'd changed her mind about being late for church, she was tromping through the water up ahead of us like this was the most fun she'd had since joining the pep squad.

When we got to the Community Pool, the three of us stood in front of the fence and stared. Sure enough, that *Closed* sign was covered up by a big piece of cardboard tacked on the fence. The rain had faded the paint, making it look like my kindergarten art projects, but I could read the words, plain as day.

POOL OPENING SOON!
HANGING MOSS PICNIC HERE
ALL WELCOME

I stared at that sign so long I thought my eyes might burn it clean in two. "What happened to make your daddy and them change their mind?" I asked Frankie.

"Maybe whatever was broken got fixed." His voice cracked and he looked away from the sign.

"Maybe something good'll come of this stupid summer and I'll get to have my pool party." I kicked water at Frankie just to see him jump.

Then, for the fun of it, Jesslyn and I started singing at the top of our lungs. We opened our mouths and let the raindrops in and the songs out. We started with "Glory Glory Hallelujah" and ended with "When the Saints Go Marching In," letting mud squish between our toes just like when we were little, playing in the backyard.

Frankie looked at us like we were crazy.

"What's the matter?" I asked him. "Aren't you happy we can swim now?" For once Frankie didn't have a single thing to say, not even a quote out of his stupid encyclopedias about how many inches of rainfall Mississippi got every summer. But Jesslyn and I kept on squishing and stomping, staring at that sign. We stopped singing when Frankie pointed over Jesslyn's shoulder.

"Hey, who's that? Driving that station wagon so slow?" Frankie crinkled up his nose and stared across the street.

Jesslyn and I turned at the same time, and of course we knew exactly who it was sitting in his station wagon with his arm hanging out the window in the rain.

"What y'all doing out here? I thought preachers' kids weren't supposed to sing on Sunday except in church." Robbie flashed that Elvis smile at Jesslyn, and right then and there, she stopped stomping in puddles.

"You're just jealous that we're having so much fun. We're celebrating," I told him. "See that sign? The pool's gonna open again."

Robbie looked at the fence gate. I saw his lips moving and another big smile start on his face when he got to the part of the sign that said *All Welcome*.

"I dare you to get out of the car," I told him. "Nothing stopping you from singing with us." Nothing but the fact that he was sixteen years old and probably thought playing in rain puddles was something you gave up way before you got a driver's license. So when Robbie Fox swung open his door, kicked his pointy leather shoes back inside the car, and stepped out, I was bowled over.

"Here's a good song for Sunday morning." In a voice Elvis wouldn't have minded one bit, Robbie belted out, "Ninety-nine bottles of beer on the wall, ninety-nine bottles of beer!" Robbie grabbed Jesslyn's hand, and we all laughed our fool heads off, marching through those rivers of water.

All except for Frankie.

When Jesslyn and Robbie ran off laughing and splashing together, Frankie stayed on the sidewalk staring into the mud. "My brother doesn't like him," he said, frowning across the street at Robbie. "He's trying to take J.T.'s place on the football team. Don't know why he had to move to Hanging Moss."

"Robbie was the star of his team in North Carolina," I said.

"The star, huh?" Frankie rubbed his arm. J.T. had popped him so hard it left a new black bruise. "So how come he didn't stay there?"

Maybe it was because Frankie looked so pitiful standing there with his socks squished down and his shoes soaking wet, with his hair slicked back and raindrops starting up on his glasses again. Or maybe it was because I was so happy the pool was opening and everything was going back to normal. But before I knew it, my words spilled out like the rain falling out of the sky.

"It's a secret why he's here. Don't tell a single soul." I looked over my shoulder at Jesslyn and her boyfriend jumping in puddles and splashing each other. "Promise?"

Frankie nodded his head. But I was in such a hurry to blab I didn't wait for him to pinky swear, which surely would have sealed the secret between us.

"Back in North Carolina, Robbie got thrown in jail. Even if it was for doing the right thing for a colored friend of his, his mama got mad and sent him here to his aunt's 'cause she was embarrassed. He even got his picture in the paper eating with his friend at a lunch counter that was only for white people." I nudged closer to Frankie.

When he glanced across at Robbie, I saw a look I'd never in my whole entire life seen on Frankie's face. It was a look of pure hatefulness. "Your sister's boyfriend has *colored friends*? He was in *jail*?"

I realized then what I'd done by telling. My heart about jumped into the mud puddle I was standing in. I should have kept my mouth shut.

"Forget it, Frankie. Pretend like I didn't say anything. It was just something I heard." I willed myself to stop telling anything more about Robbie's secret.

"You mean he's like one of those Freedom Worker people?" Frankie asked. "People messing up our town?"

"No. He's not messing up anything. Just here visiting his aunt." I grabbed Frankie's hand to make him look away. "If Jesslyn finds out I told you, she'll never speak to me again. She's just starting to be my friend again. Don't go telling Robbie's secret!"

Frankie didn't cross his heart or promise not to tell.

"I gotta go" was all he said. Then he took off down the street, and all I could think about was how could somebody who cares so much about the moon, the stars, and lightning bugs have a face that mean and hateful.

Jesslyn and Robbie were singing so loud they didn't notice me biting my lip to keep from crying. While their song went down to twenty-three bottles of beer on the wall, the knot in my stomach got bigger.

"Time for me to get outta here," Robbie said when he finished the last verse. "See you tomorrow, Jesslyn." I heard him humming all the way back to his car.

Jesslyn and I ran down Oak Street past the library, me holding my breath, praying Frankie could keep a secret. Before I knew it, we were next to the back-door choir entrance to Daddy's church. Soaking wet and barefooted. We stopped skipping and turned beet red.

Mrs. Simpson stood in front of the Junior Choir. They were decked out in white robes like a band of angels lined up to march into church. Waiting to lead the procession was our daddy, Brother Joe, with his preacher voice going. In a serious, stern tone, he said, "Gloriana and Jesslyn, get on home and change. You still have time to get to the choir loft before I begin my sermon."

We put our heads down and slugged home in the drizzle, not talking till we were at our own back door.

"Daddy's mad," Jesslyn said as we turned the hose on to wash off our feet. "I hope he never finds out about Tupelo. You didn't tell, did you, Glory?"

I crossed my fingers behind my back, which meant my lie didn't count half as bad.

"I didn't tell about Tupelo. I kept our secret."

But, well, I'd only kept *half* the secret.

The rain stopped. Sun was pushing through the clouds.

We hurried inside to put on our church dresses and slick down our wet hair.

Right about the time Jesslyn and I slipped into the upstairs choir loft together, Mrs. Simpson banged out the first notes of "The Saints of God." I looked toward the end of my hard wooden pew. No Frankie. Was he cutting church this morning?

Then Brother Joe raised up in his pulpit and beamed toward the congregation, but I got the idea our daddy wasn't exactly feeling patient and brave and true in his heart toward me and Jesslyn. "Let's bow our heads," he said, and everything got quiet.

Thinking about the pool opening, hearing the soft piano music playing, and seeing the sun shining through the church windows should have filled me up with happiness. But before Daddy could say his first Amen, I squeezed my eyes shut.

Please, God, keep Robbie's secret safe with Frankie.

Chapter Nineteen

DINNER TABLE DISASTER

Since the Lord's Day was Emma's day off, most Sundays right after the service, we'd eat with a church family. Today I hoped we'd get an invitation so Daddy would forget about me and Jesslyn sloshing in the mud. When the last hymn ended and we hung our choir robes in the closet, Mrs. Simpson started toward us. I wanted to run as fast as I could from her and that rotten-egg smile. I'd rather listen to Daddy fussing at me all afternoon than sit one single minute with Mrs. Simpson.

"Beautiful service this morning, Brother Joe. I thought our choirs sang awfully pretty, didn't you, girls?" She adjusted the hat and veil that mostly covered up her green-tinted hair. She smiled at our daddy. "Would you like to come for noon dinner? Unless someone else has spoken for you."

The next thing I knew, Lordy help us, Jesslyn and me were in Mrs. Simpson's dining room, sitting in straight-backed chairs, pushing pot roast around on fancy china plates. This was not the kind of house where anybody leaves the newspaper scattered on the floor or an iced tea glass sweating on the sideboard.

Mrs. Simpson looked down from the head of her big table like not just the Queen of the Community Pool directing her swimming Esthers, but the Queen of Hanging Moss running our town. "Brother Joe," she said. "Did Gloriana tell you she paid us a visit down at the paper?"

Just a sliver of sunlight came through Mrs. Simpson's heavy curtains and the giant chandelier over the table was turned down low, as if keeping it dark inside would make it cooler. I was sweating.

Daddy's eyebrow went up. He put his heavy silver fork down a little too hard on the white tablecloth. He looked right at me. "Is that right?" he asked.

"She brought by her very own letter to the news-paper editor, didn't you, dearie?" Mrs. Simpson took a bite of her mashed potatoes, then started cutting her roast beef. She was smiling at me as if writing to the *Hanging Moss Tribune* might just be fine and dandy.

I held on to my water goblet so tight I worried it would break. Daddy wrinkled his forehead up. He does that sometimes when he's thinking hard what to say. But Jesslyn spoke up first.

"You wrote a letter to the newspaper, Glory?" she asked. "You didn't tell me that."

I took a sip of iced tea, hoping that would settle my belly flops down. "I wrote to say I didn't think it was right to close our pool. Emma was the only one who helped me, and mostly what she did was make sure some of the words were spelled right. When I asked her to." I put my hand up to my mouth. Oh, no! I hoped I hadn't gotten Emma in trouble. I looked at Daddy. "Do you think maybe it worked? Jesslyn and I saw a sign there today saying the pool's opening to everybody."

He turned to Mrs. Simpson. "I've tried to teach my girls to speak up when they see a wrong being done. But I didn't read Glory's letter in the paper this week," he said. "That's good news about the pool."

Mrs. Simpson finished chewing with her mouth completely closed like Emma always tells us is polite, touched her napkin to the corner of her lip, and cleared her throat. "Perhaps the editor didn't find Glory's letter appropriate for our readers," she said. "And I don't know what you mean about the pool opening. Of course, my Esthers and I hate to see it closed." She patted her greenish hair and smiled. "But repairs are needed. That's that. My group will be swimming at a friend's pool. Not quite as large as our community pool, but it will have to do." Mrs. Simpson looked down the table at Jesslyn and me. "I'm sure you girls can find another place to swim, can't they, Brother Joe?"

Our daddy taught us to respect our elders. I wasn't supposed to talk back to members of First Fellowship, in particular. But I couldn't help myself.

"No, we can't find another place to swim. We want *our* pool to stay open. Did you even take my letter out of that drawer where you hid it? Did you show it to the editor?" I asked. I looked from Mrs. Simpson to Daddy, then to Jesslyn. "Somebody must've seen it. Maybe the editor gave it to the mayor. Why else do you think they put that new sign at the pool?"

Jesslyn sat up straight at the table. "If it's really opening like the sign says, I bet it was Glory's letter." Jesslyn was actually sticking up for me. "What exactly was in that letter?"

"Why, I may just have a copy right here." Mrs. Simpson pushed away from the table. She walked to the sideboard and opened a drawer. "Glory, would you like to share it since the only person who seems to have seen this is your *maid*?" She narrowed her eyes and looked from me to Daddy. She handed me the letter like it was written with a poison pen.

I took a sip of iced tea and almost choked swallowing it. I felt like I was smothering to death in Mrs. Simpson's dining room. I glanced down at the white paper covered with my best script writing. Oh, no! I shouldn't have said all that! What if I my daddy gets in big trouble? By now, my stomach was flopping so hard I could hardly hold the letter up.

But I unfolded it and began to read.

June 26, 1964
Dear Editor,

I love our Community Pool. My birthday party has been there every single summer since forever. But my forever is over now. My forever has been shut down with no plans of opening.

Some stupid Town Council committee locked the gates up tight. They claim they're making

126

the pool better, fixing cracks and broken fences. I don't believe that for a minute. They can lie all the livelong day. But they can't lock up the hot-as-fire rage burning inside me. They can hammer their Pool Closed signs, but they better not expect me to stay closed.

Does anybody think just 'cause I'm not a grown-up that I can't see everything clear as day? The people in this town dumb enough to agree to shut down a pool to keep Negroes out—and lying about it by saying it's the pool that needs fixing—they are the fools who can't see.

I hadn't lifted my eyes from that paper once. I was afraid to look at my daddy's disappointed face. My hands were shaking, but I willed myself to keep reading.

What's really broken and needs fixing most of all are the backward people running this town and the others who won't do a thing about it.

You know what? Maybe I'm the fool. And blind. Or, should I say, I was a fool who used to be blind. I was dumb enough to fall for the ugly lies. I was blind to hatred that stings more than a bucketful of the pool's strongest chlorine.

But guess what. I, Gloriana June Hemphill, can swim underwater with my eyes open. I can look through the cloudiest, strongest chlorine. And I don't blink, even underwater. I see what's going on in Hanging Moss. You ignorant people who act like you own our town aren't fooling me one bit.

I took a deep breath to slow down my heart and let the words sit for a while over the silent table. Nobody talked. Even Mrs. Simpson's clock seemed to stop its ticking.

I finished reading.

Every summer there's bothersome mosquito bites that set me to scratching all night. Sweat that makes my shirt stick to my skin. Heat that makes me nauseous. But the worse thing is when I step in a pile of what some mangy dog left behind and the mess gets all over my shoes and it stinks to high heaven.

That's what closing the pool feels like to me. Hateful prejudice and dog doo are a lot alike. They both make me sick.

Gloriana June Hemphill, age 11

My throat was burning dry when I was done reading. My knuckles were as white as the paper I was clutching. I couldn't hardly believe I'd written that! My daddy would skin me alive. But I meant every word.

Jesslyn's mouth was open wider than Mrs. Simpson's gleaming round dinner plates.

Daddy had his head down, shaking it slowly back and forth.

Mrs. Simpson looked like she'd stepped in dog doo herself.

It felt like all the air had been sucked right out of that hot dining room.

I choked back angry tears. But Daddy reached over and grabbed my hand. He squeezed it hard.

Even though I was the one crying, something in Daddy looked so sad. "I was watching your mother coming through you," he said quietly. "She was like that. Opinionated, strong in her convictions. Too outspoken to be a good preacher's wife." He laughed just a little. "You and Jesslyn remind me more and more of her every day. Your mother would have been right pleased to hear you just now. I'm proud of you, Glory."

I wiped the tears off my face, but I didn't think I could answer yet. I took a swallow of air and told myself to breathe. Then Jesslyn smiled down the table at me, and Daddy beamed at both of us, and I felt light enough to float off my chair and out of that hot, stuffy room.

Till Mrs. Simpson's hateful voice brought me right back to the dining room table when she announced, "Whatever happened to Gloriana's original letter after I shared it with the editor is not my business."

"Maybe you should make it your business, Mrs. Simpson," Daddy said. "You're on the Town Council. You could have spoken up, you know, about opening the pool to everyone."

"Many of our citizens prefer to see it closed, rather than what might happen if we allow people with germs, some who don't bathe regularly, to swim with us." She stuck her nose up in the air like she was smelling something bad. "I speak for the town, and I don't know a thing about the Community Pool opening for the remainder of this summer. Or ever again for that matter."

"You don't speak for all the town." Daddy's voice got louder. He folded his napkin and started to push his chair back. "You don't speak for me."

Jesslyn and I looked across the table at each other. That was our daddy and his choir director. Our daddy, who, while we were eating our Sunday dinners with his church people, didn't talk about more than the spring rains coming or the new driveway going in at the bank. Now here he was, standing up to Mrs. Simpson over the pool closing. Miss Bloom was right. Maybe one letter — my letter — could make a difference.

Mrs. Simpson picked up her fork and jabbed at her roast beef. Then she clanked down the fork so loud I jumped. "The pool needs repairs. There's no two ways about that. It will stay closed."

"No, ma'am." I stuck that *ma'am* in to be polite, like Emma taught me. "We saw the sign, didn't we, Jesslyn?"

For a quick minute, a worried look crossed my sister's face. "We saw a sign," she said, frowning. "It seemed real."

"A sign saying the pool's opening by July Fourth, my birthday. Frankie showed us," I said. "And his daddy's on some committee, too."

Jesslyn said, "Somebody important must've read what you wrote, Glory. I bet it'll be in the paper next week." She looked right at Mrs. Simpson. "Daddy's taught me a lot. He says the newspaper is one good way to learn what's happening in the world."

But Mrs. Simpson had crossed her knife and fork on her plate decorated with gold leaves and pink roses.

She'd folded her napkin by her iced tea glass. "The pool is closed," she said again. She rang a little bell for the maid to come take our plates, and even though I smelled something sweet as chocolate cake coming from inside the kitchen, it didn't seem like dessert was on the menu today.

"I don't believe you," I said, just waiting for my daddy to hush me up. But he didn't. Across the table, Jesslyn looked real happy to be my big sister. "My letter, that's why we'll be swimming at the Community Pool on the Fourth of July," I said. "You're right, Jesslyn — somebody important read my letter."

Chapter Twenty

IF I LIVED TO BE A HUNDRED

Laura came to my house the next morning saying Miss Bloom needed us to help at the library. I grabbed her hand and headed out the front door.

"The pool's opening up! Maybe today. Let's go see the new sign." We headed for the library by way of the Community Pool. I was talking nonstop about my pool party in five more days and how we'd have water balloon races and eat orange sno-cones and Emma's special cake, and how much I hoped she'd come. But when I saw Jesslyn and Robbie at the pool, I stopped dead still. Jesslyn squinted across the sidewalk at me. My heart sped up when I thought about Robbie's secret I'd blabbed to Frankie. But Frankie was nowhere in sight. Maybe I was safe for now.

Jesslyn stood in front of the pool sign with one hand on her hip and her nose wrinkled up. A few kids in bathing suits dry as a bone held rolled-up towels and elbowed each other. Inside the fence, nobody was splashing, belly flopping, or playing loud radios.

"What's happening?" I asked Jesslyn. "Is the pool open? Or do we have to wait till July Fourth to swim?"

"We have to wait longer than that." She pointed to the sign that said *Pool Closed Until Further Notice*.

My stomach tied itself in a knot bigger than those dry towels. "'Further notice'? What's that mean? That's a mistake for sure. We were here yesterday. If it's not open yet, it will be soon."

Jesslyn said, "Just like that busybody Mrs. Simpson told us, it was a lie that the pool would open. Nobody's admitting to putting up that sign yesterday, about the pool opening. Maybe it was a trick."

Robbie leaned against the fence, staring inside. "Your friend Frankie has a mean streak in him. *He's* the one who pulled a prank."

"Frankie?" I looked up at the new sign. "*He* did it?"

"As a joke. I heard talk, just now." Robbie shrugged his shoulders. "Some people said his brother, J.T., dared him."

I took a deep breath, smelling the chlorine and the coconut suntan lotion, trying to remember hot dogs frying on the snack bar grill, and the lifeguards' whistles. I stood between Jesslyn and Laura with the warm sunshine beating down on my neck.

"You remember last July Fourth?" I asked Jesslyn. "The watermelon race? Me and you and Frankie and our cousins at my birthday party? And that cake you and Emma made me, shaped like a cat? Remember?" They weren't really questions I was asking Jesslyn. I just needed us to remember.

"I'm sorry, Glory," Laura said.

"I don't think the Pool Committee's worried about your birthday" was all Jesslyn said.

Here I was, sure that one little part of this town had changed. That maybe people like Frankie's daddy finally got together to decide opening the pool up for everybody, just in time for a Fourth of July celebration, was the kind of thing you should do on our country's birthday. But I was wrong. My thinking was all mixed up.

"A lot of things are different this summer, Glory," Jesslyn said, the corners of her mouth turned down like maybe she wished it was last summer. "Including your friend."

"How could Frankie think tricking us into believing the pool was opening is funny?" I asked. Jesslyn just shook her head and walked off with Robbie.

When I peered through those hard metal fence links at the bluest, cleanest water, I was so mad I wanted to spit. I vowed never to speak to that hateful Frankfurter Smith if I lived to be a hundred.

Chapter Twenty-one

BALD-FACED LIE

*T*wo days later, when Frankie showed up at our kitchen door busting his britches to tell me something, I ignored him. Emma and I were reading Nancy Drew together, searching for clues in the old clock. Emma looked up once, shook her head, then turned to the next chapter.

It was the first of July, and even though I was happy that my birthday month was here, I was still red-hot-mad at Frankie. I wasn't speaking to him, no matter how hard he knocked at my door.

"Open up, Glory! I've got something to tell you!"

"I know what you did," I yelled back. "Get out of here, Frankie." I took to reading my chapter to Emma even louder.

"I didn't do *anything*." Frankie pushed open the door

and scooted his chair next to the kitchen table, but he wouldn't look straight at me.

I slammed the book shut and moved as far away from him as I could. "It was you who put up that fake sign about the pool opening. I'm not talking to you."

Emma stood and laid our book carefully on the shelf next to her cookbooks. She didn't turn to face us. Even with her back turned, I could tell she was listening by the way her shoulders hunched up.

"*I* didn't do anything. But your friend, that Yankee, did something bad. She's in trouble." Frankie looked around the kitchen. "She's not here, is she? That Laura girl. She and some of them other Freedom people committed a crime!"

"A crime? What are you talking about?" I asked.

"Laura broke into the pool and stole something."

"That's a bald-faced lie, Frankfurter Smith!"

Frankie leaned up close. His voice got quieter. "Somebody went over there last night and messed with the pool lockers. And they took candy from the snack bar. Laura and her friends did it."

"You're loony, Frankie. Laura wouldn't do that."

"Well, she did. They found one of her dumb black socks dropped on the dressing room floor." He pushed his glasses up on his nose and slicked back his hair, looked me straight in the eye like he was telling the gospel truth. "You know how you're always trying to get her to take those ugly socks off and go barefooted? This time your stupid friend did take off her socks."

Emma spoke up quietly, without turning around. "Frankie, mind your manners. Glory's friend Laura wouldn't hurt a flea."

"Yeah, Frankie. Laura wouldn't break into any old lockers. You're making that up," I said. "You're telling a lie."

"Your Yankee friend's in big trouble. There's a police car over there now. Come see for yourself if you don't believe me." Frankie took a step toward the back door just as Emma turned around fast.

Emma put her hand on my shoulder. "Brother Joe will skin you alive, getting mixed up in that mess. You're staying put, Glory."

"We won't be gone long, Miss Emma," Frankie said. "We'll just ride our bikes slow, so Glory can see. My daddy's there. We'll be okay."

Emma shook her head. "No, Glory's not going—that's that." She turned her back again to take out peaches, flour, and sugar for a pie. She started peeling the peaches.

I needed to prove Frankie was lying. I was even willing to risk getting skinned alive by Brother Joe and peeled like a peach by Emma.

I hightailed it out of there before Emma turned around to stop me.

When we parked our bikes in front of the pool, Frankie had a goofy smile on his face. Across the street was a policeman talking to his daddy. Mr. Smith had both hands on his hips and his legs wide apart. He looked like he was ready to slap somebody good. He walked right in the pool gate and slammed it hard behind him, rattling the new *Pool Closed* sign.

Frankie said, "See? Daddy's talking to a policeman. Didn't I tell you?"

"Tell me what? I don't believe a word you say. Laura wouldn't break into this pool. You don't know anything." But when I saw the policeman holding up Laura's black sock, I got an awful feeling about the whole mess.

Chapter Twenty-two

A HEAP OF TROUBLE

When I got home, I could smell Emma's pie baking. I tried to sneak back into the kitchen, but there was no getting around her. "Don't you ever disobey me like that again!" Emma was holding a pie server.

"I'm sorry. I just wanted to—"

She pointed the server at me. "Sorry's not enough. You're my responsibility when your father's away. I have a good mind to put this server to your backside."

Emma never spanked me, but oh, did she look mad now. I felt my feet ease away from her. She said, "Yes, that's right—take a step back, Glory. Step back in your thinking, too. Pause before you act, child. The sun rises slowly over Hanging Moss, and so should you."

I nodded to show her I understood.

"Go—wash your hands for supper," she said softly.

At the supper table, all of us ate quietly. I was working out how to prove Frankie was wrong about Laura. Daddy was probably thinking about preaching to the shut-ins he'd be visiting tomorrow, and Jesslyn was for sure swooning over Robbie. After we each ate a big wedge of peach pie, we headed for the front porch. Jesslyn and I pushed back and forth on the porch swing with our bare feet. Emma waited inside for her Liberty taxi ride home.

When her friend pulled up, I called out, "Hey, Mr. Miles. Emma will be there in a minute."

I stood up just when Emma stepped on the porch, and I noticed something I'd never seen before. Two little colored kids sat in the backseat of the taxi, a boy and a girl, younger than me. When the girl's eyes met mine, she looked like she wanted to wave at me, but stopped her hand before she let the wave rise up to where the open window let in this night's summer heat.

Our daddy sat off to one side of the porch holding his newspaper under the light. I leaned over to read the open page.

"Is my letter to the editor in there today?" All I saw was an ad for eggs, priced at forty cents a dozen, and an announcement that somebody was giving away kittens for free.

Daddy shook his head. "Mrs. Simpson has a lot to say about what gets in this paper and what doesn't." He turned the page. "You did a good thing, Glory."

"Anything about the Community Pool? Frankie says the Freedom Workers broke in and messed up the lockers and stole things."

"I saw a policeman there this afternoon," Jesslyn said. "What'd you hear, Glory?"

I glanced up just as Emma started down the steps. Before I could answer my sister, Emma stopped real quick and took a step back onto the porch.

A white car pulled up in front of our house. Out came Mr. Smith. Frankie was in the backseat. He didn't get out. He didn't even wave.

"Howdy, Reverend." Mr. Smith touched his hat, tipped it toward our daddy. He nodded at me and Jesslyn. He looked right through Emma like she wasn't even there. "May I have a word?" he asked Daddy.

As preachers' kids, Jesslyn and I know that when a member of the church shows up on our front porch—especially when the member is a deacon like Mr. Smith—we're supposed to give Daddy some privacy. Emma, standing with her summer straw hat set just so and her pocketbook under her arm, ready to go home in Mr. Miles's taxi, knew what she was supposed to do, too.

All three of us stepped inside the front screen door.

Daddy spoke first. "What's on your mind, James?"

Even though we'd left the porch, we could hear every word between the two men and could see them talking.

"It's about Glory," Mr. Smith answered.

"What about my daughter?"

I sucked in my breath and held it.

"You realize she's been keeping bad company, socializing with that Yankee gal over at the library," Mr. Smith said. "I heard tell Glory wrote a letter to the editor of the paper about the pool closing. Your daughter was probably unduly influenced by the girl from up North. Frankie thinks Glory knows where she's staying at."

Daddy didn't answer right off. Emma leaned closer to the door. Even without the front hall light turned on, I saw her jaw clenching and a frown taking over her face.

"We're trying to get word to that girl's mama about vandalism that occurred at the pool." Mr. Smith took a step closer. He was about a foot taller than my daddy so

Daddy had to look up at him. "Somebody broke into the pool last evening, late. Messed up the lockers and stole candy bars." Mr. Smith's voice got louder, near about made me want to cover up my ears. "We suspect it was the girl from the library."

Daddy was stretching his neck, holding his head up higher to look as tall as Mr. Smith.

"I'm speaking for the Pool Committee," Frankie's daddy went on. "But there's also people in the church who agree that Glory being friends with these outside agitators—why, she's sticking her nose in where it don't belong."

By now, Daddy looked to be as tall as Frankie's daddy. Maybe it was the sure way he was speaking.

"Well now, James. Truth to tell, I'm right proud of Glory. She's standing up for what she believes is right. All of us should lead our children to do that, don't you know?"

"What I *know* is that we can't have these *freedom people* damaging town property. We need to stand up for things the way they've always been." Mr. Smith's bald head glowed under the front porch light. His eyes looked meaner than a snake's.

Jesslyn grabbed my hand in the dark front hall.

She held it so hard I thought my fingers might break off.

I shivered.

Emma reached over and squeezed my shoulder, then hugged me close. For a minute, all I could hear was her whispering "Lord, Lord" over and over, like she was praying to herself. I leaned into her and listened to my daddy and Mr. Smith start up again. I was getting madder at every word Frankie's daddy said, but I was proud of my daddy for sticking up for me—and Laura.

"I don't believe Laura did what you're accusing her of," Daddy said. "She's visited in our home, and she is a sweet, well-behaved, polite child. She's a friend of Glory's. That's enough for me."

"That so? Well, she was up to no good last night, I tell you," Mr. Smith answered. "They found a black sock at the scene. My boys tell me she's the only person who wears those socks. She's lucky the police won't press charges—this time anyway. But her mama, that civil rights worker"—Mr. Smith pronounced *civil rights* like it was a bad taste he needed to spit out of his mouth—"she needs to know what her daughter's up to."

I couldn't wait one more minute in the dark listening to Mr. Smith. I knew I shouldn't talk back to a grown-up standing on our front porch, but that was my friend he was talking about. And this was *my* pool! And three days before *my* birthday!

I pulled away from Jesslyn and Emma, then stormed onto the porch, looked hard at Frankie's daddy. Everything, including the lightning bugs, seemed to hold still for a minute, waiting for me.

I let out a hard breath.

"You're wrong, Mr. Smith. Laura Lampert's my friend. She wouldn't do that. You're just plain wrong."

Jesslyn opened the door and stood close to me on the porch. Emma pushed by Mr. Smith and stopped at the bottom of the steps. She kept her eyes on her friend driving the taxicab.

"There's more to stories than it seems at first looking," she said. "Two sides to most stories. Folks better be thinking about that for once." And Emma kept on walking without another word 'cept to call out into the evening darkness, "Good night, Brother Joe, Jesslyn, Glory. See you all in the mornin'."

Mr. Smith shook his head and squeezed his eyes shut real tight.

"You'd best be leaving, James," Daddy said.

When the light came on in the car, Frankie was

slinking down so low in the backseat I couldn't hardly see him. Daddy held me and Jesslyn tight. "You did right, Glory," he whispered.

I didn't like the look Mr. Smith had when he stomped off our porch. There was a heap of hate swirling around Frankie's daddy.

Chapter Twenty-three

FOR DANG SURE

I needed to find Laura.

The next morning, I crept downstairs before the sun peeked over the tall zinnias blooming along our back fence. *I'm at the library* was all I wrote for Emma on my note. Pretty soon, I headed straight down Church Street.

When Miss Bloom opened the library's back door, Laura stood next to her. "Glory. You're up with the chickens."

"Did you hear, Miss B.? Something bad happened at the pool," I said. Laura had a big stack of books hugged tight and a worried look on her face. "They're blaming it on you," I told her. "Frankie's daddy came to my house last night."

"We know about the incident," Miss Bloom said. She took off her glasses, put her arm around Laura. "Laura had nothing to do with it. Everything's fine."

"That's not what Mr. Smith said." I stuffed my hand in the pocket of my shorts. "He scared me. I told him you didn't do anything. My daddy stuck up for me, too."

"You and your father are right," Laura finally said. "I didn't break into your pool. Your friend Frankie and his father are wrong."

Miss Bloom said, "Mr. Smith's just stirring up trouble. Laura was with me the night someone vandalized the pool. She and her mother and I were having supper together. I told the police that when they were here yesterday evening."

Laura looked down at her stack of books, then back at me. "I'm going back to Ohio to stay with my grandparents. They're worried. They've heard bad things might happen here."

Miss Bloom patted Laura's shoulder. "But you're here for July Fourth. And we're planning something special at the library next week. Right, Laura? A thank-you for everyone who helps with the July Fourth parade," Miss B. said.

"Miss Bloom says we'll help with that," Laura said to me.

"Something special, indeed. This is an important week for Hanging Moss." Miss Bloom's eyes squinched up and a huge smile broke out. "The parade! Fireworks! And a big to-do at the library. Won't that be fun, girls?"

Laura bit her lip like she was deciding about that.

"The library party sounds like fun. I'm not sure about July Fourth," I said under my breath.

Miss Bloom touched my hand, then looked back at Laura. "You'll enjoy the parade, all the floats. Bands are coming from all around. There will be beautiful fireworks after dark. We'll all go together. You'll be fine with me, dear."

Yeah, and the Fourth of July, day after tomorrow, was also my birthday. Nobody cared about that, that's for dang sure.

"I don't know, Miss B. The pool closing. Frankie accusing Laura of something she didn't do. Mr. Smith yelling at my daddy." I shivered in the air-conditioned library office. I hoped this parade would have the best-ever floats and bands, but the way things were going so far this summer, I didn't want to think about what else bad might happen.

"I've never been to a parade," Laura said. "It might be fun."

I bet Laura won't think sitting on scratchy grass in the summer heat with a bunch of strangers singing and waving little flags is as much fun as spending her summer finding shells at the beach like her mama had promised her.

But Miss Bloom smiled again, like all this celebrating was getting better and better.

Chapter Twenty-four

PATCHES

*I*t was finally my birthday, July Fourth.

I sat with Emma at the kitchen table mixing lemonade and cherry punch, what Frankie called bug juice. He claimed if you left it outside in the sunshine, bugs would come. But I wasn't bothering with Frankie today—as far as I was concerned, *he* was a bug, the lowest ant on earth.

"My friend Laura's going back to Ohio. She doesn't like Hanging Moss much," I told Emma. I propped my head on one hand and drew invisible circles on the kitchen table with the other. "I don't want to go to the stupid picnic. The pool's closed. Frankie's a liar. Jesslyn would rather be with her stuck-up pep squad friends, and Mr. Smith is mad at Daddy. This is beginning to feel like the worst birthday of my entire life."

Emma pulled her chair closer to me. "Want Emma to tell you a good thing happening for the Fourth of July? A special secret?"

I stirred the bug juice, not sure I needed another secret. "You mean somebody cares about our country's independence after all?"

"We got a big visitor coming to my church." Emma sat up like she was making an important announcement.

"You mean like Elvis or the Beatles? That big?" I scootched my chair closer.

Emma laughed. "Bigger." She took my hand and held it next to hers. "Mr. Robert F. Kennedy is coming to visit," she said, looking right into my eyes.

"Who's that?" I asked her.

"The most famous man in our government. He's the baby brother of President Kennedy, God rest his soul." Emma leaned in. "He's preaching about the new law, just passed. Everybody's gonna be treated the same. I'll be able to vote just like your daddy and Mr. Smith. No more white and colored drinking fountains. Everybody can eat wherever they want to. Things are changing, Glory. Mr. Kennedy's coming to prove it."

Before I could ask Emma one more thing about this famous brother of President Kennedy's, we heard a noise that sounded like the ceiling was coming down.

"Now what's your sister up to?" Emma shook her head and started up the stairs. I followed her. Jesslyn was in Mama's old sewing room, cramming shirts and sweaters into a little chest in the corner.

"What are you doing?" I asked her.

"Moving to my new room." She slammed another drawer shut. "Daddy said I could."

"You plan on sleeping there?" Emma nodded toward the little bed in the corner. "Room's too tiny for you and all your belongings. You'd be happier staying put with your sister, like you have since the day she was born."

"I need my privacy." Jesslyn pressed her lips together. "I'm going to high school soon," she said, like that explained everything. She stuffed one more skirt into her new closet before she prissed off down the stairs.

Shoot. Let Jesslyn sleep in the sewing room. I'd have more space for my books and my china horse collection and my baseball cards. But then I thought about last summer, the summer before that, and almost every summer I could remember. How we'd get under the covers to tell ghost stories with our flashlights on. All those nights we stayed up late playing Junk Poker and sharing secrets. I thought about how Jesslyn acted proud when she heard about my letter to the newspaper. How she'd held my hand when I spoke up to Mr. Smith. Seemed like she'd already forgotten about that night on the front porch.

I looked over at the sewing machine closed up in its black case, pushed off in the corner with Jesslyn's movie magazines stacked up next to it. I touched the edge of my quilt covering the bed by the window. With Jesslyn's clothes piled on top, I couldn't hardly see the quilt's pattern. I knew the squares by heart, though. Years ago, when I was little and Emma was first piecing the quilt together, I'd listen to her singing in time with the whirring sewing machine. I moved Jesslyn's pep squad jacket, sat down on the bed, and touched my quilt.

One tiny piece of the baby blanket I dragged all over the house when I was crawling.

One piece from my black cat Halloween costume.

One from my green shorts, from Lake Whippoorwill Girl Scout Day Camp last summer.

One scrap of my very first doll baby's dress.

The quilt was filled up with my life.

Now it seemed like the patches of my life were mixing into a new pattern.

Chapter Twenty-five

BLACK AND BLUE AND UGLY

By late that afternoon, I said good-bye to Emma and headed out the door, lugging the picnic basket, the bug juice, and a blanket. I walked straight to the pool and stood next to the metal fence, looking one more time at that *Closed* sign. Mr. Smith and his stupid committee had won. Nobody was jumping in the Community Pool today.

I felt like I was drowning in a freezing cold pool of disappointment and confusion. Just like swimming the backstroke when it shoots smelly chlorine into every opening on my face and sets me to spitting water, making it hard for me to get a good breath.

Outside the gate, a clown tied balloons to baby strollers. A boy riding a bike decorated with red, white, and blue streamers wheeled by, almost knocked me down. From over on the library lawn, drums and trumpets tuned up for the parade. Dottie Ann Morgan, the Hanging Moss High School homecoming queen, waved from the back of a red convertible, wearing a tiara over her beehive hairdo. I didn't wave back. She kept smiling, but she was scratching at the place where her ruffly dress's poof skirt must've been itching the daylights out of her. Some little kid dropped his cotton candy in the dirt and started bawling for his mama. A bee buzzed around my head, and finally landed in my juice pitcher. At least he had a pool to swim in—my bug juice suited him fine.

I dropped my blanket on the ground and slumped down on it. I looked for Laura.

Miss Bloom was the first to spot me. "Hello, Glory! You picked the perfect place, not too far from the library, not too close to the bandstand." She had a camera strapped around one wrist and her picnic basket balanced on the other. She spread her blanket a little ways from mine and waved to Uncle Sam walking by on tall stilts. Pretty soon Laura and her mother showed up, and Miss Bloom smiled like the world was one big happy picnic.

When I heard some girls calling out "Over here, Jessie," I turned around.

Jesslyn walked toward her pep squad friends. They had changed her name to *Jessie*?

"In a minute," she told them. She pranced herself next to me, plunking onto my picnic blanket. Robbie came to sit with us. He and Jesslyn and Laura passed around Emma's sandwiches and brownies, and I couldn't hardly believe how happy I was. "Scoot over here, Glory," my sister said, patting the space closest to her.

She pulled something from her pocket and handed it to me.

My big sister had remembered my birthday! I opened the box.

Jesslyn told what she'd gotten me before I could even get a good look. "It's a charm bracelet, Glory, just like mine." She held up her hand and jingled her own bracelet. "You can collect charms from places you visit and things you like." Jesslyn clasped the bracelet around my wrist. I rubbed a tiny silver guitar dangling from the chain. When I looked up at her, it finally felt like I was twelve years old.

"Thanks, Jesslyn," I said.

"At first the guitar was for the Beatles. For that John Lennon Beatle you and Laura are always talking about." She turned the charm toward me. "But now, it's for Tupelo," she whispered.

The backs of my ears went warm with happiness.

Robbie put his closed-up hand out to me. "For you," he said. He dropped something into my lap—a key chain with a picture of Elvis on one side and *Love Me Tender* written on the other.

"Thanks, Robbie" was all I could manage.

The band was playing "It's a Grand Old Flag." All of Hanging Moss waved their little American flags in the hot yellow sunshine and sang along.

Then that snake Frankie showed up.

I had nothing to sing about now. This day was not grand. And there was nothing worth waving at.

I walked straight over to Frankie, leaned against a pecan tree, and I glared at him.

He said, "Everything's wrong this summer." Frankie looked worried about something. There was a question in his eyes, and the start of what looked to me like tears. "Why don't those troublemakers from Ohio go back where they belong?"

I didn't care that Frankie was on the edge of crying.

I got right up in his face. "Laura *is* going back to Ohio. She's leaving. After people"—I looked hard at Frankie when I said that—"accused her of breaking into the pool lockers. She's going home."

He kept his eyes on his lanyard whistle. "It's good, then. Good that's she's leaving." But he didn't look happy about it. He looked upset.

Then he blurted, "I wish that jailbird Robbie would go back to where *he* belongs. I wish my brother would stop yelling about everything happening this summer."

I leaned in even closer to Frankie and put a firm grip on his arm. "Did you tell anybody about Robbie?" I could hardly talk, the back of my throat was burning so.

He yanked away from me and got quiet. The band's drums banged louder. Frankie rubbed at the bruise on his arm that I knew for sure came from J.T. popping him. It was black and blue and ugly.

"Why are you so scared of your daddy and J.T.?" I asked him. "Why don't you stand up for yourself?"

Frankie started to cry for real then. But I turned and walked back to my blanket.

Chapter Twenty-six

HANGING MOSS HORNETS

*L*aura, Jesslyn, Robbie, and me sat on our picnic blanket watching the Girl Scout troops and the firemen march by. Frankie had just up and left.

I taught Laura a hand clap game. *Clap-clap-knee-clap-knee-clap-clap.*

We both kept mixing up the knee-clap and the hand-clap. This made us laugh harder than hard.

Jesslyn was stuffing Emma's brownies into Robbie's mouth, two at a time, giggling. A clown handed us red and blue balloons. Maybe this July Fourth celebration would turn out okay after all.

I did a double clap with Laura to the band's drumming.

The parade was winding down. "That's the last fire

truck," Jesslyn said. "Won't be long before it's dark." She reached for the bug juice and started gathering up napkins and cups. "Let's take this to the fireworks."

But before Jesslyn could put the leftover brownies into the basket, I heard the loudest voices ever.

"Hey, you, big shot!" J.T. had his fists balled deep into the pockets of his blue jeans. His eyes were squinched tight. His friends stood behind him with their shoulders hunched up. Who'd given them an invitation to join the party?

"Having fun at the parade?" J.T. wanted to know.

Nobody, especially not Robbie, answered.

"How'd life treat you down in the pen?"

My heart jumped into my throat.

Robbie's jaw went tight. His mouth made a hard line. The boy standing next to J.T. leaned up in Robbie's face. "Yeah, Mr. Football Hero. We heard you were in jail."

J.T. and his friends surrounded Robbie. J.T. said, "Since you like eating hamburgers with the coloreds, take a taste of this." J.T. spat right in Robbie's face! His spit landed on Robbie's cheek.

They all laughed so hard. Then, as they walked off, those mean boys poked each other and laughed some more.

I'd never seen the likes of that kind of hateful.

Robbie wiped off the spit with the back of his hand. He was gripping the neck of his Coke bottle and not saying a word.

Jesslyn grabbed my arm. "Glory!" She pulled me up off the blanket and dragged me to where nobody could hear us. Her fingernails dug into my skin. Her eyes drilled a hole big enough to kill me. "Who told J.T. about Robbie?"

"I didn't tell J.T.," I said. "Frankie must've said something."

"Who told Frankie?" But the look on Jesslyn's face told me she'd figured it out. "You eavesdropped in the car going to Tupelo. You heard Robbie's secret."

My face went red. My throat was burning with trying to choke back tears.

Now Jesslyn was the one spitting—spitting angry words. At me.

"You! Little! Brat!"

She tore off, disappearing into the crowd of clowns and music and red and blue balloons.

I sat by myself, unraveling a hole in the red plaid blanket. Most everybody had moved toward the big field where the sky would soon light up with fireworks.

Jesslyn and Robbie had walked away from me without even saying a word, gone off to sit under the pecan tree. I wrapped my arms around my knees, trying to shut out what I'd done to Robbie. When I felt somebody drop down next to me on the blanket, I wiped away my tears and looked up.

Laura grabbed my hand tight. She motioned in the direction of the library. "Glory, look," she whispered.

"Well, if it ain't Elvis, alive and in person!" J.T. and his friends were back.

One of the football players yelled out, "Show him what you got, J.T.!"

Robbie pulled away from Jesslyn and stepped in front of J.T. "You got something for me?"

J.T. glanced back at his friends. "Sure do, don't we? We *all* got something for you, Mr. Football Hero."

Robbie didn't move. Jesslyn stepped closer to him. I wasn't breathing too good now. My heart was ready to jump out of my shirt.

"Shouldn't you be leaving town?" one of the football players yelled.

"Maybe you should be going back to jail?" J.T. shouted.

"Why are you still here?" called out another one of those mean boys.

So many voices hollered at Robbie, saying bad things. How was he gonna get away from them all?

J.T. took off his jacket, threw it down on the grass.

"Why'd you come to Hanging Moss in the first place?" he shouted. "Trying to take over the team? Think you're better than me?" J.T. was up in Robbie's face now. "Or did you come down here because you didn't like sharing your jail cell with a colored boy?"

I held my breath.

"Step away, J.T.," Robbie said. "No need to cause trouble."

"Trouble? *You* caused trouble back where you came from."

J.T. leaned in close to Robbie, hauled off, and whacked him in the stomach! Robbie fell hard on the ground.

Jesslyn screamed. Robbie tried to get up, but another boy pulled him down and started kicking. "See how tough you are now, Freedom Rider," J.T. hollered. "Get off your butt and show me what you got."

I shut my eyes to keep the tears away. But I couldn't stand there another minute doing nothing. I raced over and stood right next to Robbie.

"If y'all don't leave my friend alone, I'm running for the police!" I yelled.

J.T. laughed like it was all so funny. "Look who's gonna save your behind, Robbie." His voice was quiet at first and I wasn't sure what he was saying. "Little Miss Snotnose, my sissy brother's girlfriend." J.T. reached into his front pocket and pulled something out. Even standing in the near-about dark of the one dim streetlight, I could see a glint shining in his hand. Frankie's brother had a switchblade!

"How do you like *this*, Robbie Fox?" J.T. snapped the knife open. He waved it in Robbie's face, closed it quickly, then stuffed it back in his pocket. "You go home to where you came from. We don't like people trying to butt in where they ain't welcome. And we sure don't need you on our football team."

Then J.T. and his friends picked up their Hanging Moss Hornets jackets and walked away. Robbie had his head between his legs and was gulping air. Jesslyn sat on the ground next to him.

I couldn't stop shaking. "We gotta call the police," I said.

Robbie spoke slowly, like it hurt bad to talk. "Not calling anybody. No police. Can't let my aunt know."

After a while, Jesslyn and I helped Robbie up, but he couldn't walk till he'd caught his breath.

When I looked back, there was Frankie, leaning against a tree, holding his glasses in his hand. I could tell plain as day that he was blubbering. I didn't care how hard Frankie cried. He could sob all night as far as I was concerned.

Off behind the library, the first fireworks started to light up the sky in bright bursts of red and blue. Smells of cotton candy and too much butter on popcorn left over from the parade about made me throw up.

I grabbed Robbie's hand and squeezed it tight. "Come on," I said. "We need to see if Emma or Daddy's home. They'll know what to do."

Chapter Twenty-seven

GLORY BE

By the time we made it down to our house, Robbie was walking pretty good. We turned up the sidewalk, and right off Emma saw his bloody elbow and the scrapes on his cheek.

"Lord, child, what on earth happened?"

Jesslyn helped Robbie up the porch steps. "J.T. beat him up."

Emma held the front door open. "Come in the kitchen, let me look at you."

"Just got the wind knocked out of me," Robbie said, taking slow, deep breaths, then settling into a seat. "It's nothing. I'll be fine."

But Robbie wasn't fine, and Emma knew it.

Jesslyn and I exchanged glances. I was trying

to decide whether to tell Emma about J.T.'s knife.

"Robbie wouldn't let us call the police," I said. "So we came here."

Emma opened the first-aid kit. She dabbed orange medicine all over Robbie's elbow and blew on it.

Robbie flinched. He looked from Emma to Jesslyn and back again. "Nobody can know about this." He stood up like he was going somewhere.

Jesslyn put her hand on Robbie's arm to sit him back down. Her voice was full of pride. "Back in North Carolina, Robbie got in trouble for doing the right thing," she told Emma. "J.T. found out about it, about him eating at a lunch counter with a Negro friend." Jesslyn looked hard at me when she said that.

Emma leaned close to Robbie. She gave his shoulders a gentle squeeze.

Once Emma had taped a bandage on his elbow and cleaned up his face some, Robbie was in even more of a hurry to leave. "I gotta get going," he said. "My car's over behind the church."

"I'll walk with you," Jesslyn said. "You"—Jesslyn gave me a look that meant me helping Robbie was done with—"stay here."

Robbie eased himself up, real slow. He winked at

me. "Thanks, Glory, for getting rid of J.T." He followed Jesslyn out the front door.

My sister hadn't told him who had given away his secret. Knowing this all started with me telling Frankie, it made me sick inside.

"That's a big mess of trouble, that poor boy," Emma said, shaking her head.

I handed Emma the picnic basket. We folded the plaid blanket, hand to hand. I tried to think of what all to tell her. I started slowly. "J.T. and his friends didn't like what Robbie did back in North Carolina." By the way her eyes rested on me, Emma could tell I knew more.

"Might make you feel better to talk." She packed away our leftover brownies in the bread box, wiped off the kitchen table. Then she sat down and patted the chair. "Right here, Glory honey."

I spoke quietly, carefully. "Jesslyn's real mad," I said. "I wasn't supposed to tell anything about Robbie, but I couldn't keep it to myself. I told Frankie. Then Frankie blabbed to J.T. that Robbie got sent to jail." I leaned back in the chair and looked at Emma. "I'm scared."

"Those boys were wrong." Emma dropped her hands into her lap like the weight of the whole evening had just settled there. "They never should have done that. Beating up a boy who stands up for what's right. Just a heap more of the trouble that's all over the place this summer."

I told Emma how Frankie made me think the pool was open, and how he blamed Laura for something she never did. Now that I was talking, telling Emma the truth, the words spilled out fast. "The pool's closed for all summer long. I thought everything would go back to the way it was. But even if that pool opens, it'll never be the same in Hanging Moss." I stopped to get my breath and leaned into Emma's shoulder. "What's the matter with everybody, Emma?"

"Most folks just scared of losing something precious to them."

"You mean the pool?" I asked her. "The pool's precious to me."

"No, something harder to describe. Something they need to hold on to, even when they might just need a step back. Other folks, they know the best time to let go."

Emma hugged me tight, rocked me. "Almost forgot, baby." She reached into her apron pocket. "Got you a birthday present."

She handed me a wrapped box. Inside was the tiniest little book. "It's like our Nancy Drews!" I said. "It really opens and closes."

"For your new charm bracelet." She helped me snap it on.

In a minute, Daddy came in the front door. I ran to him. "Daddy, something bad happened."

"What is it, Glory? Are you and Jesslyn all right?"

"Robbie got beat up by J.T. and his friends." I looked at Emma. "They were mad because Robbie took up for some colored people back in North Carolina." Then I blurted, "J.T. had a knife."

"Where's Robbie now—where's Jesslyn?" Daddy moved toward the phone. "I'm calling the police."

"No, Daddy, please. Robbie didn't want his aunt— or anybody—to know about the fight. He and Jesslyn walked over to get his car."

Daddy's arms reached around me.

"It was all my fault," I whispered into his white shirt. "I got Robbie in trouble. I told his secret." As a minister my daddy knew a lot about keeping secrets. He didn't ask me one more question, just kept hugging me.

When Emma left to go home for the evening, Daddy held the door open and we followed her onto the cracked sidewalk. "Enjoy your Sunday blessings, Emma. We'll see you on Monday."

"No, sir. I'm coming in special, after church tomorrow, to make Glory's birthday dinner."

We waved good-bye to Emma. Then Daddy stopped for a minute and looked at me like he was just remembering what day it was. "Happy birthday, honey!" We walked back up the porch steps to sit together on our swing and watch the end of the fireworks. He and I looked off beyond the library, to where the night sky lit up with color, and bright flashes exploded above the treetops.

Daddy welcomed me into another one of his hugs. "Glory be," he said softly.

He carried his Bible and papers to his study and left me sitting, thinking about the whole day.

When Robbie's gold station wagon stopped in front of our house, the headlights went down. Jesslyn saw me as soon as she stepped up on the porch. "Why are you out here in the dark? Go inside."

I put my feet down to stop the swing. I stood up and reached in my shorts pocket. "I'm sorry about tonight, Robbie." I handed him the *Love Me Tender* key chain. "You can have it back. I don't deserve your present. It was my fault J.T. beat you up. I blabbed your secret to Frankie."

Robbie wouldn't take the key chain. "Jesslyn already told me. But I don't care about J.T. I don't need that kind of trouble. After all that's happened, I'm leaving. To live with my mother again."

"What about football—and Jesslyn?"

"Robbie called his mama tonight. She's coming tomorrow, early." Jesslyn's voice was so soft I wondered if I'd heard her right. She leaned her head on Robbie's arm. She was crying, even more than before. "Who wants to stay where people are so horrible to you?" she was asking into the warm night. Jesslyn kept on talking, speaking to what seemed like only herself. "Robbie has promised to come visit me," she said.

But I couldn't see Robbie Fox spending another minute in Hanging Moss.

Chapter Twenty-eight

A TORNADO WENT THROUGH

I sat on the top stair, touching my new charm bracelet, thinking about how to make Jesslyn happy again.
I looked down the upstairs hall toward the sewing
room. That's it! The sewing room! I snatched up all
the clothes Jesslyn had piled on the daybed. I ran to
our old bedroom, dropped her favorite blue sweater on
the way, but I kept going. I went back for her basket
filled with makeup and hair rollers. I stuck her fancy
tasseled boots in the big closet in our old room. My
Nancy Drew books and china animals were lined up
in perfect order where they'd been ever since I could
remember. I carried them to the sewing room. My
room now.

Next, I grabbed my Buster Brown shoe box. What

did I need with that silly stuff—Cracker Jack prizes, a rusty skate key, my Jacob's ladder string?

I dropped every last piece of my old junk, one by one, in the wastebasket. When I got to the dried and crumbly grass from Elvis's house, I put it back, next to the two shells I couldn't bear to part with. Then I came to the faded pool notice, the lie Frankie had written about the pool. I wanted to rip it to pieces, but I folded it into a hard triangle and put it in the box as a memory of my twelfth birthday in Hanging Moss.

I didn't want to forget everything.

I waited by the window, holding my breath till I heard Robbie's car drive off and Jesslyn starting up the stairs. When she stormed into the bedroom and flung her blue sweater onto the bed, I jumped a mile.

Her voice was low, but she was sure mad. "Who did this? Who destroyed my new room?" Jesslyn looked around and saw her hairbrushes and boots and mascara, all in our old room.

"Emma's sewing room is plenty big for me," I told her. "You're the oldest. You get the biggest room."

Jesslyn stared at the two beds, all the windows, the closet that my entire new room could almost fit into, like she couldn't believe it belonged to her now. "You're giving *me* this room?"

"All yours," I told her.

Jesslyn got so still I thought maybe she was mad. "Robbie made me promise to forgive you for telling Frankie his secret."

"I'm sorry he's leaving, Jesslyn," I said. We were both real quiet. "Wanna play cards?" I asked.

"You mean Junk Poker?"

"I dumped my junk out, same as you. Didn't think you'd ever want to play again. I'm putting new things in my shoe box, to save forever." I held up my box and started to untie the purple ribbon. "Wanna play Junk Poker with our new stuff?" Jesslyn could tell by me not being able to look at her that deep down I hoped she'd say no. I didn't want to bet my new treasures.

"We'll play Double Solitaire," she said. I put down my shoe box.

Jesslyn laid out her cards on the bumpy bedspread.

I turned over a queen and looked for a place to play it. "The pool's not opening again, is it?"

Jesslyn smoothed out the bedspread, then added a nine of hearts to her cards. "Things won't ever be like they were before, Glory."

I flipped over three more cards but nothing was working on my side. "Miss Bloom says in a few years, everybody'll be wondering what the fuss was all about. I hope she's right," I said.

Jesslyn put down her last card and beat me, but this time she didn't brag. "Sleep in here tonight." She moved a pile of clothes from the extra bed. "In my room, with me," she said. "We'll clean up tomorrow. Your new room looks like a tornado went through."

Chapter Twenty-nine

A SMILE AS BIG AS MISSISSIPPI

The next afternoon, Jesslyn was upstairs listening to Elvis and mooning over Robbie. Daddy was resting after church. Emma was in the kitchen fixing my birthday dinner and wearing the prettiest blue dress ever.

"The table's set," she said. "Everything's ready for your special day—well, one day late." She laughed at the face I made over that. "And the cake! Icing's there for you and Jesslyn to put on together. Chocolate, your favorite." She held up a big yellow bowl.

"Thank you, Emma." I peeled back the waxed paper and stuck my finger in the bowl. She swatted at me, but she smiled, too. "Did you hear? Robbie's gone," I said. "And Frankie might as well be." I licked icing off my finger. "That awful Old Lady Simpson, she didn't speak to me or Jesslyn at church today."

"Don't you be worrying about folks like Mrs. Simpson—don't give her the satisfaction. The world doesn't change by magic, baby. But we'll get there." She took off her apron and reached for her fancy hat.

"Wait, Emma!" I pulled her back close to me at the table. "You didn't tell me about Mr. Robert Kennedy. Did he come to your church today?"

"He sure did, Glory honey. The church was filled to overflowing. Everybody was there. It was like nothing I've ever known before." She settled back in her chair. She held up her hand, the one with the slim gold ring that never left her finger and she'd promised to give me when I grew up. "Hold my hand, baby," she said. "You're touching the hand that touched Mr. Bobby Kennedy."

"Now *I've* come close to somebody as famous as a president." I threaded my fingers through Emma's. "Somebody important. That's one good thing about this summer."

"You know, Glory," she said. "By making your friend Laura glad to be here, you're somebody important, too." She held my hand right up against hers. "Don't you worry. We've got powerful praying hands, don't we?" She winked, then hugged me tight. She smelled like cake with chocolate icing. Like the pine soap she'd scrubbed the saucepans with. I buried my face in her blue dress and took in all her goodness.

I thought for a minute. "Emma, I figured out what's got people like Mrs. Simpson and Frankie's daddy so riled up. It's not just the new people in town. It's things changing so fast that's scaring them. When people get scared, they make up lies. They keep secrets. And they act mean."

"You've learned a lot, baby."

"When this summer started, I never thought I'd know a real secret."

"Real secrets mean more than hiding that card game from your daddy. Real secrets can be hurtful. Make people do bad things." Then she hugged me again. "No matter what, you know Emma loves you," she whispered into my hair. "See you tomorrow, Glory."

Then I remembered. "Emma, Miss Bloom said to invite you to the library tomorrow."

Emma drew her breath in real quick and took a step back. "What for?"

"The thank-you party for everybody who helped out

at the July Fourth parade," I said. "You made a whole lot of food for the picnic. You get invited."

Emma nodded her head. "Well, I just might do that, Gloriana June Hemphill. I might just come to a party at the library."

"You can bring anybody you want," I said. "Miss Bloom said to tell you that, too."

She patted her hat on and headed toward the front door. "I bet you had something to do with this fine invitation." When Emma said that, I felt like I'd grown a whole foot taller since turning twelve yesterday.

I looked right at her and sent a smile as big as Mississippi. "Don't forget, Emma. I'll see you tomorrow."

Chapter Thirty

BOOKS DON'T CARE WHO READS THEM

The next day, I tucked my ironed shirt into my shorts, fastened on my silver charm bracelet, and headed to the library.

Down near the end of the street—of all people—J.T. and his daddy waited under the library's big shade tree. A police car pulled up and Mr. Smith leaned in to talk to the officer. J.T. moved closer to the front library door and crossed his arms like a statue guarding the place. I ignored him and marched right up the sidewalk.

"Hey, Miss B."

Miss Bloom waved back at me, and the handful of balloons she was holding almost floated to the clouds.

"Come on in, Glory. Lots left to do," she said, and we hurried inside.

The library looked downright beautiful! Miss Bloom's flowers filled the tops of the lowest shelves. A fancy new poster at the checkout desk explained how to sign up for a library card. This afternoon, even the air in the library felt different.

"Who's coming to this shindig?" I asked.

"We invited the mayor," Miss Bloom answered. "All the library board members, anybody who helped with the July Fourth celebration. That big sign with the balloons out front is welcoming new library patrons." Then she leaned in so close I could practically read what was written on her dangly book earrings. "Is Emma coming?" she asked quietly.

I didn't have time to answer before the front door slammed wide open. In pranced Mrs. Simpson, dressed up in her white gloves and high-heeled shoes, trailing her Esthers behind her. All those ladies wore big hats, disguising their green hair.

"We're here to help," Mrs. Simpson announced. She jerked her head from side to side, probably looking for *undesirables* she could keep out of the library, like she claimed she'd done for the pool. Miss Bloom handed them a stack of paper napkins and trays of cookies and pointed to the tables in the back of the library.

"Glory, you and Laura are in charge of the children's room. Laura's there waiting for you."

When she heard Laura's name, Mrs. Simpson stopped in her tracks and wheeled around fast. She took off her white gloves, carefully folded them into a pocket of her pink plaid skirt, and said, "I thought only those citizens who'd actually helped, had volunteered for the July Fourth festivities, were invited to our library today."

"Since Laura arrived in Hanging Moss, she's been helping me," Miss Bloom said. "And this afternoon's event is also to welcome new library users into our community."

"New? As in people who've never read a book before? Don't know why they'd need a library." Mrs. Simpson smiled and bobbed at her Esthers.

I looked right at those ladies and said, louder than I should have, "Laura's mama is coming, too. Right, Miss B.? With all her friends. They all like to read."

Mrs. Simpson pranced off with her nose in the air. Miss Bloom looked at me and rolled her eyes before heading back to the checkout desk.

I wanted to grab Mrs. Simpson's big straw hat and

stomp on it. Before I could do a thing the door opened again, and my worst enemy, Frankfurter Smith, slipped in. What was he doing here? Frankie hardly ever set foot in the library. Claimed everything he needed was in his very own set of encyclopedias. I didn't have time to follow him before the front door opened wide again.

Emma! I raced over to welcome her to my library for the very first time.

"You came," I said. Behind her was a boy and a girl, her friend Mr. Miles from the taxi, and another lady I didn't know. She and Emma were dressed up just like Mrs. Simpson and her friends.

"So this is the library?" Emma beamed at me. "This is where you spend all your days. Beautiful!" The boy and girl hid behind Emma, peeked around her skirt. "This is my neighbor, Mrs. Williams." Emma nodded toward her friend in the blue hat. "You know Mr. Miles and his taxicab business. And these two rascals"—she pulled the little boy and girl around in front of her—"they're Mr. Miles's children, Regina and Eddie, and they love to read. Just itching to get their hands on books."

I waved at Regina and Eddie. "Hi," I said softly.

Miss Bloom came around the corner, smiling as big as you please. "Welcome, everyone," she said. "Glory, take those youngsters right into the children's room. You and Laura can help them fill out the forms for library cards."

Before I could do a thing, the door opened again and in came J.T. Smith. He looked around the library like it was a fancy ballroom he'd mysteriously stumbled into.

Well, Mrs. Simpson must have heard all the commotion. She marched around the front tables, busting her britches to see what she was missing. When she saw Emma and her friends, she stormed right up to Miss Bloom. "May I speak to you in private?" she said.

J.T. took one step closer to Miss Bloom, but she stared him down and he backed toward the door. She turned to Mrs. Simpson.

"Let me introduce you to Mrs. Emma Moore and her friend Mrs. Williams. Those cookies you're serving probably came from Emma's oven." Miss Bloom's smile reached around to all the ladies.

You can bet Mrs. Simpson was not about to shake hands with Emma or her colored friend. Didn't look like she ever wanted to see Miss Bloom again, either. She looked straight at Mrs. Williams in her nice dress and pretty hat with flowers on it, then down at the two children behind them. "If I'd known you were inviting just anybody, Miss Bloom, my friends and I would have stayed home. Or insisted the library close."

Emma smiled at Old Lady Simpson, but I could tell it was a fake smile. I bet she wished she had a pie server in her hand to chase her out the library door.

Muttering about *Yankee troublemakers* and *Negroes,* Mrs. Simpson stomped off.

"Why wouldn't she speak to you, Emma?" I asked in a quiet voice.

She looked from me to Miss Bloom and shook her head. "Folks like that think they're better than anybody else, but she's not. Mrs. Williams here and me, we know we're as good as anyone. It doesn't matter if those ladies never talk to people like me."

Miss Bloom's lips made a hard line. "This is not right. Mrs. Simpson will see. What's next on her list? Closing schools? Our park?" She stopped to let that sink in.

Even before Daddy showed up, this day was turning into a mix of sweet and bitter. But when he opened the door, he seemed calm as the afternoon breeze. That is till Mrs. Simpson stopped him cold.

"Your girls," she said, pointing a long, skinny finger at our daddy. "It's a shame they have no mother to teach them to behave. Being raised by a *maid* is no way to learn what's acceptable and what's not. I don't recall them acting this way until these outsiders moved in and Glory befriended them. And welcoming *new people*"—she narrowed her eyes at Emma and her friends—"into *our* library? As far as I'm concerned, this library should be closed, too."

"That will never happen, Mrs. Simpson. Never," Daddy said. "Libraries are about books. Books have no color. And they don't care who reads them."

Miss Bloom moved closer to him and nodded her head so fiercely her earrings were a blur. Mrs. Simpson stormed out of the library and vanished down the sidewalk. When the door opened, I saw J.T., Mr. Smith, and the police car had disappeared, also.

Emma stepped over to me and reached for my hand. My smile and my heart were both about to crack wide open with happiness.

Chapter Thirty-one

WHAT ALL I LEARNED THIS SUMMER

*M*aybe it was the balloons out front or Emma's famous lemon cookies that caused the library to fill up. But with all those people, I couldn't find Frankie. I looked behind the big globe next to Miss Bloom's desk. Nope. Not near the cookies, either. Emma and her friend waved to me from the mystery book section, but I didn't expect to find him there.

Frankie had disappeared.

Laura was still in the children's room. I plopped myself near her in a big chair. "Whew! This is hard work," I said. "You seen Frankie? He's steering clear of me today."

"He was here. Explaining what actually happened at

the pool break-in," she said quietly. "He even apologized about stealing my sock."

"Frankie apologized?" I sat up in my chair. "I'm really sorry about the lies he spread, Laura."

"I think he meant it. I really believe it was mostly his brother's fault," Laura said. Then she smiled and handed me a present. "For your birthday," she said.

I peeled off the tissue paper. Two books of stamps and two little packages of blue note cards she'd decorated with music notes tumbled out. "We'll be pen pals," Laura said. "One for me, one for you."

I remembered what I had in my pocket. "So you won't forget this summer." We passed the small shell from my Junk Poker box back and forth, sharing the sound of the ocean.

Laura's mama walked up about then, with her friends from the clinic. Pretty soon, there was a line at the checkout desk waiting for new library cards. And those very same chairs Miss Bloom had vowed would never be removed to keep anybody from coming here and sitting awhile? They were filled with people reading newspapers and books, including Mr. Miles and Regina and Eddie. Next thing I knew, Miss Bloom was *tap-tap-tap*ping, ringing the little bell at the checkout desk. Emma and Mrs. Williams moved from the mystery books toward Miss Bloom. I stood next to Emma and reached for her hand again.

"Welcome to the Hanging Moss Free Public Library," Miss Bloom said. "We are so honored to have you all. Thank you for your hard work on the July Fourth celebration." She stopped to look around the big room filled up mostly with happiness now. "We're especially glad to see those of you who are new here. We hope you'll come often." Miss B. leaned behind the desk and reached for something. "We have scrapbooks in the library, filled with memories. Today, I'll add to them."

Miss Bloom stepped into the room and started snapping photographs. The instant kind you wave around till they dry and everybody comes into focus. She held one up. "Maybe we'll send this picture off to our newspaper," she said. "Show them what this town is really about." Then Miss Bloom winked.

It was right at me.

For the rest of the afternoon, Miss Bloom smiled almost as bright as the big yellow sun shining through the front picture window. Her library was filled up with people who loved books.

But I still needed to find Frankie.

I peered around tall shelves into a corner of the children's room. Who *was* that? Frankie? Spread out on the floor with Regina and Eddie? The *F* encyclopedia was wide open.

He turned the pages real slow. "Fireflies light up at night to attract prey," Frankie was saying. "They mostly live in warm climates, like Mississippi. You ever seen lightning bugs? Same thing as fireflies. Really they're beetles, you know."

I tiptoed quietly away so I wouldn't disturb his explaining the life cycle of a lightning bug.

Laura and her mother said good-bye. Emma and her friends headed home. But Frankie ducked out without saying a word. On the chair where I'd been sitting in the children's room was an envelope with my name on it.

I opened it and out fell a fluffy pink flower and a picture postcard of the soldier in front of the County Courthouse. On the back of the card was a note.

Dear Glory,
Please meet me at Fireman's Park tomorrow. I'm still sorry about all the bad things that happened.
Your friend (I hope), Frankie Smith

I squished the pink mimosa flower between my fingers, trying to get the same smell as when we climbed the tree together. But really, I needed the whole tree blooming to get the sweetness out of the blossoms.

Even if we sat under our special tree again, I wouldn't tell Frankie what all I learned this summer. But I didn't hate him. Emma had helped me figure out what hate really and truly was. That wasn't how I felt toward Frankie.

By now, most everybody had left. I put things away with Miss Bloom. "Scoot along home, Glory. You've been a big help," she said.

Outside, the sky was turning a million colors of purple and blue. It smelled like it might rain any minute. I wished I could show this to Laura Lampert. I bet she never sees colors like these in her big-city sky in Ohio.

Jesslyn waited for me on the sidewalk. We took the long way home, past the Courthouse and park, by the water fountains where I'd first seen my friend Laura do something I never dreamed of doing.

"Miss Bloom says those *Whites Only* signs will be gone soon," I told Jesslyn.

"Good riddance," she answered. I nodded and kept walking.

"Let's go by the pool," I said. "Just in case."

We both knew that pool was shut up tight. It wasn't gonna open this summer. Maybe never. But it didn't hurt to check.

"Closed," Jesslyn said, almost without looking at the padlocked gate.

I leaned close to the pool fence and gazed one last time at the empty lifeguard chairs up high above the blue water. I took a deep breath to remind me of the times I'd sat under that mimosa tree with Frankie.

"You know what, Jesslyn? When this summer started, I worried that the worst thing would be the pool closing before my birthday and me not having a party. Being twelve is turning out okay after all." We crossed Main Street together and I said, "We still have that mess of a room to clean up. Before Emma sees it and gets after both of us."

"Maybe I'll find some barrettes. Do something about your hair." My sister flipped my ponytail and made a face.

We both laughed at that. Then we headed back down the cracked sidewalk, walking fast toward home.

Author's Note

This is a work of historical fiction. It is based on reading and research, interviews with friends and family, and especially on my own memories. It is a made-up story, with some very true parts.

Seeds of *Glory Be* were planted the summer I was a college student working in the Mississippi Delta home-town where I was born. The library where I interned was almost shut down by a very vocal trustee who didn't want "just anybody"—which meant anybody who wasn't white—using the books. Like Miss Bloom, my librarian didn't let that happen.

That same summer, another librarian introduced me to a young white civil rights worker from Ohio who spent a lot of time in our Bolivar County Library. Her story wedged itself into a memory crevice, ready to emerge in the form of historical fiction. Many years later, I imagined that teenager as Laura Lampert.

My sister and I made up the game of Junk Poker, and I was probably as bossy as Jesslyn. I actually visited Elvis's little Tupelo house before it became a shrine. Like Glory and Emma, I read every single Nancy Drew book with my beloved Alice. My own daddy was not a preacher but, like Brother Joe, he taught his children a lot about right and wrong.

When Robert Kennedy came to my hometown in the spring of 1967, he toured the black neighborhoods and spoke to the editor of the local newspaper. I took liberty with the truth and changed the date to fit my story.

In 1964, the town I lived in did not have a public swimming pool. Neighboring towns, however, did have pools that closed. With the goodwill of local ministers, librarians, teachers, and other community leaders, my town managed to keep our Fireman's Park and our public school system open and intact.

My white friends and I who grew up in Mississippi and spent Freedom Summer in the South agree that, unlike the sisters in my story, we only really understood much later the events that swirled around us.

I once thought this book was about sisters, how they

grow apart and come back together. Then smart, important people showed me it was about more than sisters. Still, I would not have remembered the details of the summer of 1964 without my own sister and my friends who became part of the telling. Although I lived in the middle of the most impoverished part of the South during very turbulent times, I wish I could say I was Glory or Jesslyn. Gloriana June Hemphill and her sister were braver than I ever knew how to be.

There's a saying that "Mississippi grows storytellers." I was raised with stories told around the Sunday dinner table. Most nights, my grandmother dreamed up new bedtime tales for us. English teachers and librarians introduced me to the very high bar set by my state's great literary heritage. Since I was old enough to listen, I've been hearing Mississippi in my head. This is one story I needed to share.

Acknowledgments

My favorite Mississippi writer, Eudora Welty, wrote: "It doesn't matter if it takes a long time getting there; the point is to have a destination." Although she had in mind a sea voyage, I believe that applies to writing books. I had a lot of help reaching this destination.

My New Jersey critique group—Leslie Guccione, Kay Kaiser, Ann Bushe, and Lee Hilton—listened to my early, false starts. I owe them apologies as well as thanks. Leslie saw a glimmer of a story she loved in a very early draft and passed me along to Barbara O'Connor. For that journey, I'm eternally grateful.

My Florida critique groups piloted me through the midpoints. I listened especially to the logic and creativity of Janet McLaughlin, Teddie Aggeles, Melissa Buhler, and Sue Laneve. I'm glad I did.

At the beginning of my trek, Margaret Gabel and

her New School students laughed at the right places and showed me the way. Joyce Sweeney, another gifted teacher and editor, pushed me toward the finish line.

Without the Society of Children's Book Writers and Illustrators, this book might still be languishing in a bottom drawer. Close to my destination, I met an amazing agent, Linda Pratt, at a regional Maryland SCBWI conference. She made the connection between me and my remarkably brilliant editor, Andrea Pinkney.

Although I tapped into the online oral history collections of both the Library of Congress and the University of North Carolina library, I also discovered nooks, crannies, and countless interlibrary loan opportunities in branches of both the Pinellas County, Florida, and the Morris County, New Jersey, library systems. My original research was done at the Bolivar County Library in Cleveland, Mississippi. A huge thank-you to my fellow librarians everywhere.

Southern friends dropped everything to answer my frequent, frantic questions. Is it iced or ice tea? Cut off the light or turn off the light? And the larger question: *Could this really have happened this way, at this time?* For their diverse, helpful answers, I am eternally grateful to Mimi Clark, Eileen Harrell, Beverly Jones,

Patty Horsch, Ivy Alley, and Jane Carlson. Although we all lived through the '60s in the South, we each had our own experiences. Their collective memories as well as long hours with books by and about Mississippians inspired me, but I made up the story.

—Augusta Scattergood